Poor Law

By

R J Lynch

Book 2 in the James Blakiston Series

Published by Mandrill Press www.mandrillpress.com

ISBN 978-1-910194-22-5

Chapter 1

The graves were unmarked, but he knew which they were. In truth, they were hardly graves at all. The bodies had been so young, and so undernourished, and anyway no pains were taken over the likes of them. Paupers' children. The undeserving poor. Too lacking in God's grace to know his blessings, here on earth or in the life beyond into which they were so soon projected. Of course, where there was no money there were no headstones, no crosses, no physical markers of any description but there had once at least been mounds where the earth had been heaped over the dead. Now the mounds were flattening, the earth sinking back into the spaces left when worms ate the flesh and the woollen shrouds decayed.

Buried in woollen, as the law required; better dressed in death than ever they had been in life because a woollen shroud was less expensive than the five pounds fine if no affidavit was recorded in the parish register. The cost of a pauper's burial was born by the parish and the parish was not going to pay fines that could be so easily avoided.

The graves were not side by side; they had not died at the same time and others, equally unworthy, separated them, but he knew which they were. Oh, yes. He knew which they were.

He knelt now beside the grave that held the first child to die and laid a flower where he judged the heart might once have been. A single rose from the hedgerow. Red. The colour of blood. The blood of one of those who had destroyed his family. There would be more.

Blakiston was finishing breakfast when the message came. 'Ned Greener,' he said. 'What brings you here so early, and in such hurry? Is all well at Chopwell Garth? Sit down, man, and break bread with me.'

'I cannot, sir. Our Tom says you must come immediately.'

Blakiston raised his eyebrows. Placing his last piece of ham on his last piece of bread, he put the last of his cheese on top and the whole thing in his mouth. Then he washed it down with the last of his tea, as Ned hopped from foot to foot and looked repeatedly at the door. Blakiston wiped his mouth with a linen napkin sent in with his breakfast by the inn. 'And now you may tell me,' he said, 'what is so urgent as to make Tom Laws so forget himself that he gives orders to his landlord's farm agent? Even if I am soon also to be his brother-in-law.'

'Margaret Laws is dead, Master.'

Blakiston cast his mind over the members of Tom's household. 'Margaret Laws? But there is no Margaret Laws.'

'Joseph's wife, Master. Joe that is Tom's brother. She is murdered.'

Blakiston rose to his feet with such haste that his chair fell backwards to the floor. As he reached for his broadcloth coat, adjusted his wig and donned his tricorn hat, Ned restored the chair to its upright position.

'Leave that!' barked Blakiston.

'But sir...a chair...'

'Is only a chair. Get to the door so I can lock this place and we may be gone.'

Blakiston saddled Obsidian, the black stallion that was his only vanity. Ned was already astride the nag that still trembled from the unaccustomed speed of its journey from Chopwell Garth. When Blakiston rose into the saddle, Ned turned to lead the way.

'Take care,' said Blakiston, 'or you will kill that poor beast. Ride beside me. I must hear this tale before we arrive.'

'I shall tell you what I know, Master, but that is not much. Joseph Laws came this morning, and a more piteous sight I never saw. He had been in Carlisle on some errand and he did not reach home

5

till the sun was up. He found Margaret dead on the floor. Strangled, Master.'

'And what of the others in the house? The maid? The child? Margaret had a child, had she not?'

'Aye, master. A boy, Samuel. As to the maid, I do not know. She was away out.'

'You think she killed her mistress and fled?'

'Who knows what women will do, Master? When Joseph returned home, she was not there; and that is all I know.'

'So he has left the child with his mother?'

'They buried her three month back. It was the consumption that took her, not four weeks after her husband died. Our Tom was that cut up about it.'

'He was. I remember now. But the child can scarce fend for itself. Joseph Laws brought his son with him to Chopwell Garth?'

'Nay, Master. He was in such distress he left the bairn alone in the house. Our Kate is gone to tend to it.'

'Kate? Kate is alone? With a murderer about?' Blakiston dug his heels into Obsidian's flanks and surged effortlessly away from Ned's poor mount.

When Ned reached the end of the lane to Chopwell Garth some time later, Lizzie Laws waited open-mouthed for him.

'Mister Blakiston is here?' Ned asked.

'He galloped straight past,' his sister replied. 'You told him our Kate was alone at New Hope Farm, did you not?'

Still gasping from his pursuit of Blakiston, Ned could only nod.

'Then that will be where he is.'

Blakiston found that Kate was not, in fact, alone with two-year-old Samuel for Susannah, the New Hope maid, was with her. That did not stop Blakiston from telling this young woman he loved so completely, but who to his anguish was re-examining her promise to marry him, that she should not be in such a place without company.

'I had not realised I was invisible,' said Susannah.

Blakiston turned his head. 'Do not be pert with me. You are under suspicion in this matter.'

'Me, sir?'

'Yes, *you*. Where were you when this dreadful thing happened? Why were you not here, about your master's business?'

Ample chest heaving, Susannah said, 'I was visiting my mother. I do so every Friday night. It is an arrangement I have with Mistress Laws. Had with Mistress Laws,' she corrected herself.

7

Blakiston stood closer to her. 'Well, I cannot verify that with her, can I? And I'll thank you to address me properly.'

The maid looked down. 'Yes, sir. I am sorry, sir.'

'Margaret is in the dairy,' said Kate. 'Would you like to see her?'

'She was killed there?'

'She was killed here, in the kitchen. We have moved her body into the dairy, where it is cool.'

'Did you not know I should have liked to see it where it lay?'

'But here is her child. Would you have had us leave his mother in his sight? Let me take you to see her. Susannah will stay here with the bairn.'

'I am the maid here,' said Susannah. 'Am I to do as I am told by a farm labourer's daughter?'

'If that cause you distress,' Blakiston said, 'then *I* instruct you to remain. Are you content now? The body, Kate, if you please.'

To reach the dairy meant crossing the yard. As they did so, they saw Ned turn up the lane towards them.

'That poor horse is on its last legs,' said Kate. 'But Tom will not hear of it going to the knacker as long as the breath of life is in it. He almost killed it when he attacked the press tender on its back, but he has a tenderness for it, for he believes it helped bring him and Lizzie together.'

'Bring them together? But they had been married more than a year by that time.'

Kate looked as though she had more to say but thought better of it. 'So they had. I do not know what I was thinking of.'

'It is well that Ned is here for he can come with me into the dairy and you may be spared seeing the body.'

'James! I have *seen* the body! It was Susannah Ward and I who carried it from there to here. With no man to shield us from the horror. Though the horror is in your mind only, for a body is but a body. Once the soul is safe in the arms of Our Lord, the body is but an empty shell.' She smiled. 'You were upset on my behalf that it was me who found poor Matthew Higson's body, were you not? And that was nought but bones, while poor Margaret still looks like a plump farmer's wife.'

'Plump? I thought her a skinny thing.'

'Yes. Well, you shall see.'

Ned had no need to rein in his mount, for when it reached them it simply stopped. 'You had better give that wretched horse a drink,' said Blakiston. 'Before it falls to the ground beneath you. Then go into the kitchen and keep a close eye on that woman in there until Kate and I return. I shall wish to question her more deeply.'

In the dairy, Kate laid her hand on Blakiston's arm. 'James. May I speak openly?'

He looked down into the calm grey eyes she shared with the rest of the Greeners. 'Of course, Kate. But first you may tell me why you do not wish to call me by my name, or act as though we are to wed.'

'Oh, James.' She took a deep breath. 'It is only in front of others that I call you Mister. No-one could love you as I love you. And I know you love me. But you are gentry and I am not, and we have not yet fixed the date for the wedding...'

'...because *you* will not...'

'...and I am afraid it will never happen and *then* where will I be?'

'But my love, of course it will happen, and as soon as you say the word.'

'Really? And who will marry us? The Rector? You see? You do not answer, because you cannot. You and he were such good friends and now you do not speak to each other at church. And please do not tell me that is nothing to do with you and me because I know better.'

'Mister Fawcett will marry us. The new curate.'

'And I shall be happy. But will you? You are giving up too much by marrying me...'

'...I am gaining the world, Kate...'

'...and if you will not protect yourself then mebbes I should. And what about your family? Do they want you marrying someone who says "mebbes" when she means "perhaps"? What have they to say?'

'My brother is delighted for me. If he is on shore when we wed, he has promised to be my Groom's Man.'

'And your sister?'

Blakiston said nothing.

'You see? James, there is marriage and there is marriage. We don't have to go in front of an altar. We can stand in the church gate, hold hands and leap together over a broomstick with the curate as a witness. That way I don't get any right to what's yours but in the eyes of God and the church we are still married.'

'Kate. I want us to be husband and wife.'

'But we would be.' She smiled. 'And even if I can't get my hands on what is yours, you will still have the freedom to put yours on what is mine.'

'Kate!'

She hung her head, but her smile came up to him through the white folds of her cap. 'You see? I am too rude to be a gentleman's wife. You would be better with Susannah Bent. And she certainly thinks she is the woman for you.'

'Susannah Bent?'

'Do you not see her in church on Sundays? Casting down her eyes and yet still looking at you? I never knew till I saw Susannah Bent doing it that you could flirt while seeming not to look at the person you are flirting with.'

'Good Lord. I have been to dinner three times at the Bents' house. The daughter sat next to me each time.'

'And you never suspected a thing. James, you are too good for this world. And too innocent.'

'Let us forget Susannah Bent. You are everything to me and she is nothing. And you said it yourself: there is marriage and marriage. And I want to know that the world respects our choice. And that will not come from leaping over a broomstick like a pair of witches. If I want it and you want it, what do the Rector and my sister matter? But, please. We can continue this later. A woman has been murdered, and you wished to tell me something.'

'I did. I do. It is about the way you speak to Susannah Ward. Do you remember, when Reuben Cooper was killed, how certain you were that Matthew Higson had killed him? And how you went on believing it, until poor Matthew turned out to have been murdered himself? By the same hand that slew old Reuben?'

Blakiston coloured. 'You believe I form my judgements too quickly?'

'That is not for me to say. But Susannah did not kill Margaret. I would stake my life on it.'

'I find her absence questionable.'

'It is usual for a maid to be given an evening off each week.'

'Yes. I suppose that is true.'

'Susannah is loyal to this family. She came here as little more than a child. She skivvied here when our Tom was still living with his mother. I think she hoped that Joseph would one day take her for his wife, and she would become mistress of this farm when Tom's mother died.'

'You dig her grave more deeply with every word!'

'No. She had accepted her disappointment. If you question her mother as to Susannah's whereabouts last night...'

'...and you may be sure I shall...'

'...then I think you will find that Susannah was not with her at all. Or not all night, at any rate. She walks out now with Jemmy Rayne. Tom's cousin. And Jemmy, you know, has a farm of his own.'

'I know Rayne. He is a good man. He did an errand for me once to Staithes. It put me on the trail of Reuben Cooper's killer.'

'I did not know that.'

'And I should not have told you, for Tom arranged it and he swore me to silence. You must forget what I have just said.'

'I shall. But, you see, Susannah will be mistress of a farm of her own one day soon, and so she has no need to kill another farmer's wife to clear her path.'

Blakiston's voice was gruff. 'You think she lay with Rayne last night?'

'I believe she will be more careful than that. It is the farm Susannah wants, not the farmer. To be mistress in her own house, and not the maid. And she knows farmers. Once they have milked a cow, they move on to the next. But I see I have embarrassed you again.'

Blakiston's face was indeed bright red. 'Do not go dropping one of your curtseys, Kate. I do not believe I could bear it. What a calculating hussy she must be.'

'No, James. Not all men are decent and loving like you. Susannah knows how many maids have been got with child by their masters, and then thrown out to fend as best they can. I am sure she will be as good a wife to Jemmy as Jemmy could ever hope. Once they are married. Shall we look at the body?'

'You see I did not exactly mean plump,' said Kate.

'How long had she been with child?'

'I cannot say. We knew nothing of it at Chopwell Garth.'

'You did not see her often?'

'Every Sunday, at church. But she went about in a loose bedgown that came down to her hips. The babe did not show.'

'There were no visits between the two families?'

'I will not say none. But they were few. Joseph is not a gadding about man, and neither is Tom.'

'They like each other?'

'Well enough. I never heard Tom say a bad word against his brother.'

Blakiston raised the dead woman's arm. 'It is stiff.'

'She was limp when we carried her here.'

'That is something that happens when people die. After a while, they become hard as this table she lies on. Then they soften again. If I knew how long it took, we might make some kind of guess as to what o'clock she was killed.' He took the watch from his waistcoat pocket and looked at it. 'It is now eight fifteen. I must remember that when I ask the doctor this question.'

15

'Better ask the animal doctor. Doctor Barraclough knows nothing of the human body, except that his works better when it is filled with whisky. Or you could speak to the Rector. Priests see more dead people than doctors do.'

'I believe you may be right.'

'Except that now you do not speak to the Rector at all. Because of me!'

'See how livid are the marks upon her throat. I do not think there is much doubt but that she was strangled.'

'If you have seen all you want to see, I should like to undress her and lay her out. It would be respectful.'

'Is that really a proper job for you, Kate?'

'I hope you are not going to say that I am too young, or too innocent?'

Blakiston smiled. 'Perhaps I was. I am sorry. It would not be decent for me to be here. I shall look at the place where she was killed, and question that ill-tempered woman.'

Kate watched him cross the yard towards the kitchen and wondered, for perhaps the thousandth time since he had proposed marriage and she had accepted, what the future could possibly hold.

Chapter 2

Blakiston knew that Kate had spoken no more than the truth when she suggested he jumped too quickly to conclusions. He had received the credit for finding the killer of Reuben Cooper and Matthew Higson, but as he had said to Rector Claverley, "I made many mistakes," and one of those mistakes had been to prejudge what was important and what was not. "Next time," he had said, "I shall follow everything until I know it has no bearing on the case, instead of deciding in advance what matters and what does not." The Rector had smiled at the idea that there would be a next time, and Blakiston himself had expected that this "next time" would be investigating the secret he felt sure Dick Jackson carried within himself and not in yet another murder. But here he was. Excitement tingled his scalp. Someone was dead, unlawfully killed, and this time he would get to the root of the matter more quickly than he had before. This time, when people said he had done well, it would be true. This time, he would deserve the praise.

'Show me where you found your mistress,' he said to Susannah.

The girl pointed at the floor some distance away. 'She was there.' After the slightest pause, she added, 'Sir.'

'Come, Miss. Am I to be pouted at by a maid? Move to the place and show me.'

The slowness with which she slouched across the floor was a calculated insult, and Blakiston knew it. 'She was here. Sir.'

'You try my patience. Shall I have Rayne thrown off his farm? Would he thank you for making me angry?'

'Sir...you would not...you must not...'

'That is twice today someone has told me what I must and must not do, and dinner time not yet here. Let me tell you what *you* must do; you must answer my questions with haste, with politeness and with truth. Otherwise it shall go badly with you and those close to you. Am I understood?'

'Yes, sir. I am sorry, sir.'

'Then let us make a fresh start. Where did you find the body?'

'Here, sir.'

'And how was it arranged?'

'Well, sir...it was...I know not how to tell you, sir.'

'Ned. Go to the place. Now put yourself on the floor. Get on with it, man. Thank you. Now, Susannah Ward, arrange Ned so that he is as you found the dead woman. Ah, Kate. You have finished laying out the body already? That did not take long.'

'No, I have not finished, but I have found something I believe you should see. But what on earth are you doing with Ned?'

'He is representing the dead woman so that I can see where she was before you moved her.'

'Would you like me to do so in his stead? For I am a woman, as poor Margaret was, and I saw how she lay.'

'Of course. Ned, get to your feet and allow Kate to take your place.'

Ned's relief was clear, but Blakiston was soon to regret agreeing to the substitution, for between them the two young women arranged Kate in a way that draped her petticoat high above her knees and gave him his first sight of a thigh as perfect as his besotted mind might have expected. 'Yes, yes,' he blurted. 'You may stand up now, Kate. You said you had something to show me? It is in the dairy?'

'Did you see how Susannah Ward glared at me?' said Kate when they were again alone with the dead woman.

'Pah! She is of no consequence to me.'

'But she must be to *me*.'

19

'Then tell her we are to be married.'

'Not until we have fixed a date, please. I shall be the talk of the parish.'

'Kate, you are worth ten Susannah Wards. One hundred. More. Put her out of your mind.'

Kate hung her head and clenched her fists by her side. Blakiston was beginning to recognise these signs of rebellion. 'Now,' he said. 'What was it you wished to show me?'

The girl sighed. When she moved to the bench on which Margaret Laws lay, Blakiston was unwilling to follow her. 'Please do not be concerned for your modesty,' she said. 'I have made sure the poor woman is decently covered. But look here.'

She had removed Margaret's bedgown and the petticoat it covered and taken off the large neckcloth the woman had worn like a shawl. Apart from the cap on her head, that left only the shift and Kate had torn that downwards from the arm hole just enough for Blakiston to be able to see the dead woman's side. He said, 'She has been beaten as well as strangled!'

'So it would seem. What I asked myself was, where was she when this happened?'

'But my dear Kate, how can we know?'

'I will show you. Suppose you wished for some reason to beat me.'

'But, Kate, I would never...I *could* never...'

'We are merely supposing. Let us suppose a little further. Suppose you were a complete stranger. A burglar, let us say, who thought there was no-one here. What do you suppose I would do, a weak and defenceless woman, faced with this desperate ruffian? A ruffian who knows if he is caught he will hang, or at the very least be transported to Virginia?'

'Why, Kate, I suppose you would run.'

'I suppose so, too. And what would you do when you saw me try to escape?'

'I should come after you.'

'And then?'

'I should catch hold of you.'

'Then let us see.' She turned her back on Blakiston. 'I shall pretend to run away from you, and do you run after me and catch me. And then pretend to strike me, as the supposed burglar struck Margaret.'

'But Kate, I could not...'

'We are merely pretending, James. But what is needed is for you to try to strike me in the very place that her bruises show Margaret was struck.'

'Ah. Yes. I see. Very well, Kate; you may consider me a desperate ruffian indeed. Attempt your escape.'

Kate lifted her petticoats from the ground, giving Blakiston a thrilling glimpse of slim ankles, and began to run across the dairy floor. He caught her with ease, his left arm going around her throat to pull her firmly against him. For a moment he breathed in deeply, allowing her scent to fill his nostrils and revelling in the sensation of her firm young body pressed against his. Then he raised his right hand in a fist and prepared to swing it into her ribs. He paused.

'Kate. I cannot.'

'But we are only pretending. I am not asking you to hurt me.'

'What I mean is that while I am in this position I cannot strike you in the place where Margaret was struck.'

'Aha. You see? This is what I supposed. But change hands, and let us see what difference that makes.'

'Change hands?'

'You are right handed. Perhaps the man who killed Margaret is left handed.'

'Of course.' As Blakiston moved Kate's throat from his left arm to his right, he was acutely aware of what she must feel pressing against her. 'You have never wished for hooped skirts, Kate?'

'That is a foolish fashion, and not for the likes of me. Though I can see how they might spare a gentleman's blushes at a time like this.'

'Kate!'

'Am I to curtsey again? Or shall we forget for the moment that we are a man and a woman who love each other and get on with what we are about?'

Blakiston swung his fist, holding it back before it could make contact. 'No. With this hand it is even less possible.'

'So Margaret was not hit from behind. Let go of me and we will see how it may appear from the front. Now. Place this hand on my shoulder...yes, like that...and bring the other fist up to hit me here. Yes! You see?'

'She was hit from before.'

'So she was looking at her attacker, and not trying to flee from him.'

'She knew her assailant!'

'It seems possible, does it not? And now let us look at the marks on her throat.'

Blakiston turned to the body. 'What do they tell us?'

'You see they are at the front. There is nothing behind.'

'So she was still facing her murderer when she was killed. But how can we know she was beaten before she was strangled?'

'And not strangled before she was beaten? Is that what you mean?'

'Yes. How can you be so sure?'

'I cannot. But I am picturing the scene in my mind. After she was strangled, she was dead. She would have been lying on the floor. He might have kicked her, the rotten bully...'

'But not punched her. Yes, I see. You are right, Kate.'

'And, see. The marks are high on the throat. She was looking up at him.'

'He was taller than her!'

'Or he had thrust her to the floor. Or he was taller than her *and* he had thrust her to the floor. For, see, if you will look at her poor knees you will see that they are scraped and there is blood on the surface. And that is all I believe the body has to tell us. I shall finish laying her out, and if I see anything else that may interest you I shall say so.'

'Thank you, Kate. You have been a most instructive assistant.' He turned towards the door but Kate called him back. 'There is one other thing...'

'Yes?'

'Before I closed her eyes, I examined them closely. There is no image to be seen.'

'What?'

'You know they say that a murdered person keeps the image of the murderer in her eyes, where anyone who looks may see it.'

'Where do you hear such tales, Kate? That is arrant nonsense.'

'Well, you may be right. For I have looked and there is nothing there.'

Chapter 3

Watching Blakiston ride off, Kate felt that she was being left to face the music alone. It started as soon as she came back into the kitchen from the dairy.

Susannah Ward said, 'I am the maid here. You came, you said, to mind the bairn. Though I was here and could look after him as well as you. Better, for he knows me and he scarce knows you. But here you are, and then yon overseer comes and you leave the boy in my care and gan off to the dairy with this man who I must call sir, or Master, but you it seems need not.'

'Be quiet,' said Ned. 'What there may be between Kate and Mister Blakiston is no business of yours.'

'Oh, you admit it then?' said Susannah. 'There is something between them, this man and your harlot of a sister?'

The speed of Ned's hand in striking Susannah astonished Kate. The maid was taken completely by surprise and she fell to her knees. With a coolness she did not feel, Kate crossed the floor and took the screaming Samuel from the maid's arms. Susannah stared at Ned. 'By God,' she whispered, 'but you will pay for that.' And, at that very moment, the kitchen door opened and a plump man in clerical attire walked in.

'What is happening here?' asked the new curate.

Susannah was on her feet in an instant, a hand rising to stem the flow of blood from her mouth where Ned had slapped her. 'Oh, Mister Fawcett, it is God's providence that you are here. There has been one murder already in this house, and you arrived just in time to prevent another.'

'You stupid woman,' said Kate. 'The only danger you were in was provoked by your own mouth. Did you think you could slight me in front of my brother?'

'Come now,' said Fawcett. 'Am I to stand here and listen to two fishwives trade insults? I have the Rector's calash outside. Kate Greener, you are to bring the babe and come with me to Chopwell Garth, where I shall leave you. Susannah Ward, the constable will be here directly to question you about your part in last night's doings.'

'I *had* no part in...'

'Do not raise your voice to me, Miss. You, Ned Greener, will wait here. When I have reunited Kate and Samuel with their family, I shall return with the carter and you will help him put the body of Margaret Laws onto his dray so that he can take her to the church, where she shall be prepared for a decent Christian burial. Is all clear?'

All three nodded. 'Who gives these instructions, Mister Fawcett?' asked Susannah.

'I do. Did you not hear me?'

'I meant, who gave them to you?'

'The constable, of course.'

'The *constable!* The constable is Jeffrey Drabble. He was elected because he is a labourer who knows his place. And now he gives us orders.'

'They were not his orders. He spoke to Rector Claverley for guidance. But Jeffrey Drabble will be in charge until we know how Margaret Laws died, and by whose hand. You would be wise to treat him with the respect due his office, if not his person. Come. Let us begin. Kate Greener, get to the calash with the bairn. And by all that's holy, try to shut up that infernal noise. I cannot bear the sound of a baby crying.'

When they were in their seats and heading for Chopwell Garth, Kate asked, 'If Jeffrey Drabble is in charge, what is to be Mister Blakiston's part?'

'I have been here a short time only, and there are many things I do not yet know, but I think our constable is not a fool. And, you know, he is merely a constable.' Having said this, Fawcett fell silent, as though he had answered Kate's question.

'But what is to be Mister Blakiston's part?' Kate repeated

'Whatever he wishes it to be, I should say, subject to Lord Ravenshead's wishes. It was Mister

Blakiston, I understand, who had my predecessor taken to Durham Gaol?'

'It was. But George Bright was the constable then.'

'A dissenter. That was very irregular. When he was chosen, he should have appointed a deputy.'

'Everyone liked George Bright. After him we had William Stevenson, who was not liked and I cannot say why he was elected. And now we have Jeffrey Drabble, and people are happy once more.'

'Well, Jeffrey Drabble should not have been elected, and once elected he should not have been sworn, any more than George Bright should have been. Constables must be honest, understanding and able men, which from what I have seen of him Drabble may be, though he is passing old for the duties of a constable, but they should also be men of substance, which Drabble is not, and not of the meaner sort, which he undoubtedly is. By God's good grace, a petty constable has very little power. He has only to preserve the peace, search for common nuisances and execute warrants. So the answer to your question is that Mister Blakiston is Lord Ravenshead's farm overseer and if his lordship does not object then of course Mister Blakiston may pursue the killer of Margaret Laws as he did Martin Wale. A constable is only a constable. The gentry are the gentry.'

'What is a common nuisance, Mister Fawcett?'

'A common nuisance may take many forms. Some may say that a pretty girl may never be a common nuisance, but I would say that a pretty girl who will not stop asking questions can be exactly that.'

To take the sting out of his words, the curate turned to look at Kate and smiled. Then he laid his hand on her petticoat, quite high up on the thigh. One look at the expression that appeared on her face and he instantly removed it.

Chapter 4

When Jeffrey Drabble had finished his interrogation of Susannah Ward, he came to tell the Rector what the maid had said. Why he did this he did not know, except that the Rector had suggested he should and he knew that independent thought was not prized in a petty constable.

Drabble was both relieved and made anxious at finding Blakiston with the Rector. He had not forgotten the concern of Dick Jackson that Blakiston might somehow uncover the long-forgotten matter of the Dobson boy and, as Jackson's cousin and oldest friend, he did not want to be interrogated on that question.

The two men were neither speaking to nor looking at each other. Each held a glass of port. Claverley was smoking a clay pipe. No refreshment was offered to the constable, and nor was he invited to sit down.

The Rector's welcome, though, was cordial enough. 'Mister Blakiston is about to tell me what he has learned from his examination of the body, Drabble. He does so because I am a Justice of the Peace. But you are Constable, and had better hear what he has to say, before you give your report.'

'Our most interesting discovery,' said Blakiston, 'was that whoever killed Margaret Laws was in all likelihood known to her.'

'Our?' said Claverley. 'You were not alone?'

'I had most estimable help from Kate Greener,' said Blakiston. 'Indeed, I think I should not have learned what I did without that young woman's aid.'

Claverley's eyes flickered at the mention of Kate, but he said nothing.

'Sir, how could you tell that Maggie Laws knew her killer?' asked Drabble.

Blakiston was about to reply when the Rector interrupted him. 'I do not think you should refer to the dead woman as Maggie. She was a farmer's wife, and you are a labourer who might from time to time be employed by her husband.'

Drabble had turned bright crimson. 'Beg pardon, sir.'

'There is more than one Mistress Laws, so for convenience you may refer to her as Mistress Margaret. But the question is good. What told you this, Mister Blakiston?'

'It is not something we can be certain of. But the position of the blows to her body, and the marks on her throat, tell us she was looking at her assailant, and indeed looking up, when they were inflicted. Had a stranger been involved, she would surely have been running away.'

'You did well to notice those things.'

'I can claim no credit. Kate Greener drew them to my attention.'

Once again, the flicker in the Rector's eyes said that he might have pursued this question of Kate Greener, but he did not. Instead, he turned to Jeffrey Drabble. 'And your interview with the maid, Susannah Ward. What had she to tell you?'

'Nothing of use, your reverence. Only that she arrived home on the stroke of six this morning and found the door standing wide open, her mistress dead on the floor and the bairn still asleep in his bed. There was no-one else in the house. I asked how she could be sure of the time, for she has no watch, and she said she had heard the church clock as she walked up the lane.'

'I see you have a watch yourself, Drabble.'

'Yes, sir. You see it has three seals.' He held it out proudly towards the two men for a moment before he noticed the Rector's disdainful look and hastily pushed it back into his jacket pocket.

'What did she do when she found such carnage?'

'Well, sir, I imagine she screamed. Her being a young woman, and a show-off.'

The Rector stared at Drabble in silence for so long that Blakiston fidgeted in embarrassment. Drabble reddened again. 'Sir, she ran out into the fields to look for help.'

'Why the fields? Why not into the village?'

'That would be some distance by the road, your reverence. It was already light. She knew there would be men working. She found William Snowball not half a mile from the house.'

'Snowball?' said Blakiston. 'The Snowballs are squatters, are they not?'

'Squatters may be respectable people,' said Claverley.

'I think I must question him, nevertheless. He was close by the place where a woman was murdered. But go on, Drabble. What did Snowball do?'

'Why, sir, he ran to Ryton to tell me. He is not recovered yet. All the Snowballs run to fat, sir.'

'And Susannah Ward?'

'Returned to the house, sir. To tend to the bairn. Who was out of bed when she came, and downstairs, and trying to wake his dead mother. Sobbing his little heart out, as Susannah tells it.'

'There was no sign of Joseph Laws at this time?'

'Well, sir, that's the thing of it. He had been home and found his wife dead, and run to Chopwell Garth to raise the alarm.'

'Leaving his son of two years alone in the house.'

'Yes, sir.'

Blakiston shook his head. 'That is the part I cannot understand. But proceed. Snowball is running hither, and Joseph Laws is running thither. What came of all this running?'

'Sir, there is no more. What I was able to discover, I have told you.'

'Very well,' said Blakiston. 'The next thing, Drabble, is that Joseph Laws himself must be questioned. But I think you had best leave that to me.'

When the Constable had gone, overseer and rector sat in silence for a few minutes. Kate Greener's name had made it impossible that either of them could forget the conversation they had had so recently, when Blakiston called on Thomas Claverley to tell him that he proposed to marry.

Thomas had made no attempt to hide his disapproval. 'She is beneath you, Blakiston. Think what you are doing.'

'I have thought about it, Rector. Long and hard. I am in love with Kate Greener and I mean to marry her.'

'In love! Were ever two more foolish words joined together? Oh, Blakiston. I have watched the girl grow up. She is beautiful, I know. More beautiful than any child of Ryton has a right to be. I know not where her beauty comes from. But beauty deceives, Blakiston. Beauty ensnares. A wife is not only someone to look at. A wife is not only someone to lie naked in your arms. No, Blakiston, I see your anger but I will be heard. I owe it to you. I owe it to our class.

'Who will you have to talk to when you come home weary? Who will raise your children as people like us would have them raised? Who will you know? For it is sure no gentlefolk will receive you when this foolish marriage takes place.'

'Reverend, you make me speak as I would not. Forgive me, but I am trying to understand the difference between Kate Greener and your own wife.'

Claverley fell silent. Then he said, 'It is true that Lady Isabella is of common stock. But her father had raised himself, Blakiston. When I married her, she brought me a thousand pounds a year.'

'So. I ask your forgiveness again, Rector, but what is it that qualifies a woman to raise our children as what you call people like us would have them raised? Is it a pedigree of many generations? Or is it a thousand pounds a year? If Kate Greener had money, would you no longer make objection?'

The Rector's mouth was a tight, small line. 'There is no talking to you, Blakiston. I do not wish to call your banns.'

'I will have you do so.'

'I will not. The curate shall do it. You are about to make a dreadful mistake. I wash my hands of the matter.'

'I believe there is precedent for that in the faith you preach each Sunday.'

'Blakiston, I have no more to say to you. I shall bid you good day.'

That was how it had been. Two men who had been close friends were driven apart by the desire of one to marry and of the other to stop him. Nor had the rector left it there. Blakiston wrote to his sister, Hannah, that same evening, telling her of his good fortune and inviting her to the wedding. He saddled Obsidian and rode to the Crown, a coaching house in Chester-le-Street, to ensure his letter caught the first available post. He could not know that his was not the only letter his sister would receive from the same town.

Hannah's reply had come more swiftly than Blakiston would have thought possible.

Cromer Castle. 20th August 1764

Dear Brother

Having had no letters for many months, I was surprised to receive two on the same day. Your own, and one from Rector Sir Thomas Claverley who you know. He tells me that you are to make a dreadful mistake and that all his wise counsel can not dissuade you. I must hope, for my own sake, that I have more success. Certainly you may count on me to speak frankly, whatever the cost to my pride.

Forgive me if I say that it seems to me that it is always men who behave foolishly, and always women who must live with the result. It was a man, our father, who ruined my life with his unwise dealings. Now it is you, my brother, who is to condemn me to spend the rest of my days in penniless unhappy slavery.

You wish to marry. You say your Kate is the sweetest girl under Heaven and that you are the luckiest man alive. James, I implore you to think what you are doing – to me, if not to yourself. This girl has bewitched you. It is she who will think herself the lucky one – lucky to have cast her spell over a man she is not fit even to look at from afar. You will be cast out from Society. Your wife will be received in no polite home, for she is a girl of the basest origins and you have neither the money nor the position to force people to accept your choice.

This may mean nothing to you now, in the heat of your passion. Then think of me, dear brother. I was born into a good family, with every expectation of an acceptable marriage. Perhaps, even, to a man of title. Now, because through my father's errors I bring no portion, I am forced to waste my life caring for the unpleasant children of a woman leading exactly the life I should have led. For this I receive thirty shillings on the first day of each year, and a new gown every six months. And I am expected to curtsey and look grateful for it. I take my meals in the schoolroom with the children. I rarely enjoy adult conversation. The very housekeeper looks down on me!

I long for our brother to be raised to the rank of Captain, and for there to be a war, so that he may earn the prize money that will enable him to buy me out of my wretched station. Each time a new man visits this house, I examine him minutely. Is his fortune too great for him to notice me? Or is it possible that my salvation may have just entered my life? If, that is, I can contrive a situation where he even meets me. To make matters worse, Sir Thomas tells me that you were offered marriage into a good family and that the woman in question, one Grace Hodgson, was not only handsome but possessed of an income of five hundred a year. Did you think of me when you turned down this alliance? Did you think that I could have come to live at Hoppyland Hall with you and your new bride, free of the tyranny of the small children of others, until I found a man of my own to marry? The rector even tells me that your bargaining position was such that you could have demanded a dowry for me. I cannot tell you how long I cried when I learned what you had refused.

Love is not for our class, James. Love is for the poor, the labourers in the fields.

Look how little good it does them and
you will see what regard God has for it.
And now in your mean-hearted
selfishness you wish to make the whole
family into lepers, so that your sordid
lust can be sated with a village girl who I
make no doubt would allow you all the
liberties you desire with no need to
venture near a parson. Jamie, I beg you. If
you will not save yourself for your own
sake, do so for mine.

I long to hear that you have been restored
to your senses. If not, know that I shall
not attend your wedding. Nor shall I ever
again refer to you as my brother. I shall
cut you from my life. If your name is
mentioned I shall deny that we are of the
same family. In my helplessness and need
I can not do otherwise. I have written to
Peter. Doubt not that he will take the
same line as I.

I close in desperate hope.

Your sister

Hannah

Blakiston had sat over the letter, reading it again
and again. Then he had torn it into small pieces
which he had scattered to the winds.

Blakiston missed the Sunday night dinners he had enjoyed each week at the rectory, but he saw no solution. Had Jeffrey Drabble not sought instructions from the Rector, he would not have gone there to discuss the murder. But here he was, and his presence reminded him that the loss of this friendship hurt.

'You have taken it on you to solve this murder?' asked Claverley. 'So soon after the last? What has his lordship to say?'

'We have not yet spoken on the matter. But how could I not? The dead woman is the wife of a tenant on one of the estate's farms. Anything that harms it harms us.' He raised his head and stared directly at the Rector. 'And she was the sister-in-law of the woman I intend to wed.'

Thomas answered his stare. Then he stood, walked round his handsome escritoire and stood by the window, hands behind his back, staring out into the warm August afternoon. 'And what has his lordship to say on *that*? I take it you have spoken of your planned folly to the man who employs you?'

There was a sharp knock on the door, which opened immediately. Thomas raised his head to shout at the intruder, but closed his mouth quickly when he saw that it was his wife who stood in the doorway.

Blakiston stood up and bowed his head. 'Lady Isabella,' he said. 'It is a pleasure.'

'Is it, Mister Blakiston? Is it really? Then perhaps you will tell me, for it is certain that my husband has not and will not, why it is that we see you no more for dinner on Sunday nights?'

'I...I...' Blakiston looked for help to Claverley, who shrugged and turned away.

'Is it the soup?' asked Isabella. 'Are you tired of Rosina's way with a fish? Has she bored you with too many puddings? Be sure she wishes to know.'

'Lady Isabella. Please. The food here has always been a delight, and you may tell Rosina so.'

'Then it is *us!*' cried Isabella. 'Me, or Thomas here. We have offended you. But please, tell me how? And what can we do to correct our wrong?'

'Isabella,' said Thomas. 'These are men's matters.'

'Ah!' said his wife. 'The important matters of men, too deep and too weighty for a poor woman to comprehend. Then let me tell you what I do understand, husband. I understand that a friendship that brought you great contentment is over, and that you are miserable. I understand that my task as a wife is to look after my husband and to remove those things that prevent his happiness when it lies in my power to do so. I understand that something has come between you and Mister

Blakiston and that you are sadder as a result. What I do not understand is why you will not tell me what it is.'

The two men looked at each other in silence. Then, in flat sentences from which he could not hide the sadness or the anger, Blakiston said, 'I am in love. I wish to marry. Your husband does not approve.'

'He would keep you single? He wishes you to continue your Sunday visits? Your bride would refuse to grace our table?'

'He would not countenance her presence as a guest in your house.'

Isabella placed a hand over her mouth. 'You would marry a papist?'

'I am engaged to marry Kate Greener.'

There was silence. Isabella looked from one to the other and back. The two men looked away, out of the windows. Eventually, Isabella said, 'Mister Blakiston, I wish to speak to my husband. I do not know whether your business with him is done, but if it is not I will thank you to come back and finish it tomorrow.'

When Blakiston had left the room, Isabella did the same. Thomas called her back. 'You wished to speak to me.'

'I do. I shall. When I have understood what I have heard, we shall speak. When I have truly got into my head the fact that my husband would reject a close friend because he loves a woman my husband does not approve of, we shall speak. Until I can understand these matters, which I confess, husband, at this moment defeat any attempt I may make to follow where your thoughts have gone, I have nothing to say to you.' And off she went.

Dinner that night in the Rectory was eaten in something close to silence. John hurried into the kitchen to tell Rosina of the obvious rift between their master and mistress, and to ask whether the cook knew what might have caused it. Rosina had no explanation to offer.

After dinner, Isabella left the table without a word. The Rector finished his claret and went into his study where he poured himself a glass of Madeira and lit a pipe of tobacco. There was no further contact between husband and wife. The clock struck ten. He heard John locking, chaining and bolting doors and windows. Thomas would inspect the work before he retired, for that was his task, but he knew the rectory would prove as secure as it had always been.

Fifteen minutes later, he heard Isabella's footsteps on the stairs as she went to bed. Usually, she would pause for a moment to knock on his door and bid him goodnight. She did not do so tonight.

Thomas did not want to go to bed until he was sure Isabella would be asleep, but his candle was burning down and he would soon be unable to see. He carried it into the hall, which was in darkness, and then into the kitchen. John the manservant, Rosina the cook and Sarah the maid all had rooms on the top floor, which they reached using their own staircase, and the scullery maid slept on a sort of truckle bed which was placed on the scullery floor at night, and so he hoped to find no-one up, but John was at the kitchen table.

'I thought you would be gone to bed by now.'

'Sir, I had not heard you check the locks.'

'I will do it. Go to bed. Wait. Find me a new candle. Then go to bed.'

Back in his study, the new candle providing a comforting light, Thomas lit a second pipe of tobacco. He waited until the clock had struck eleven. Then he waited ten minutes more. Isabella would surely be asleep by now.

He examined the locks, and then went up the stairs as quietly as he could. In his dressing room, he undressed without a sound and put on his nightshirt. Then he blew out the candle, made sure it was completely extinguished, opened the door to the bedroom he shared with Isabella and slipped quietly inside. Treading carefully, he crossed the floor, drew back the bed coverings and climbed into bed. He left as much room between himself and Isabella as he possibly could without falling onto the floor. He was tired and longing for sleep. He closed his eyes.

'And now,' said Isabella, 'you may tell me exactly why you are treating Mister Blakiston in this dreadful way.'

Lady Isabella usually wrote her journal in the evening, when dinner had been eaten, their daughter was asleep and there were no other calls on her time. She began this entry immediately after breakfast.

> *Thursday, 23rd August, 1764*
> Really, I am not prepared to set down the
> reasons Thomas gave me for his break
> with Mister Blakiston, for they were not
> reasons at all. For as long as the history of
> people has been known and talked about,
> men and women have fallen in love.
> Sometimes, their families have
> intervened to prevent marriage taking
> place. Among the well-to-do, love has not

been what decided whether two people should marry. Love is not what caused Thomas and I to wed, for when our parents arranged our match we had not even met.

But love is a beautiful thing, and Mister Blakiston has no parents alive to decide how he should live, and Kate Greener is one of the finest human beings in this parish, poor though her family may have been before Wrekin's ravishing of her sister Lizzie brought Lizzie marriage to a farmer so that Lord Ravenshead's illegitimate granddaughter should have a decent place to live.

Nor are we like the French, who draw such rigid lines between aristocracy and peasantry. It has always been possible in England to move from class to class – I am an example! Why, Lord Ravenshead is another, for he is a baron but his father was a baronet and, if he looks back but three generations, he will see a family only raising itself into the middling sort. And <u>why</u> do those who have money and position resist marriage of others of their kind with those who have them not? It is because they are afraid! Not of the poor themselves, though they have that fear too and that is why the Law has such dreadful penalties to keep the poor in subjection. No; what strikes fear into their hearts is the knowledge that money may be lost and position may be transitory. The poor remind them that they, too, may one day go from wealth to painful necessity.

I told these things to Thomas, and he cried. I felt so moved when I saw the tears come. For Thomas had taken his stance as a defender of Society's laws without thought, and the loss of this friendship has caused him such grief. I had intended to tell him that he must give in and marry Mister Blakiston to Kate but I had no need. For Thomas said that this was what he wanted to do, but that he had seen no way to retreat from his foolish position and make his peace with Mister Blakiston. And he said that he would do it, and that he would do so on Sunday. I promised to help him. Thomas was so happy to have given up his stubborn foolishness, and I put my arms around him and we held each other close, and I felt signs that he had other wishes that might be satisfied. And then I had an idea. I told him to wait for a moment and I got out of bed and went into my dressing room and put on the drawers I made after I heard of Mistress Wortley's daring but never had the courage to wear myself. I shivered with excitement when I thought that I might be, after her, only the second woman in Durham County to wear drawers. And then I thought, "How can I know that? How many women are setting themselves free to excite their menfolk in this way?" And <u>then</u> I found myself wondering who the widow Wortley had meant to please, and I realised it was herself alone. And I resolved to be more attentive to pleasures that are for me and not for my family. But that will be difficult to put into practice, for it goes against everything we women are taught from our girlhood. Be that as it may, I lit a candle and carried it into the bedroom and said to Thomas, "What do you think of my new garment?"

Thomas's reaction was all I might have hoped, if not more. And very soon the drawers that I had only just put on were taken off again. And I hope that what we did then will have reminded Thomas that there is more to marriage between a man and a woman than adherence to Society's rules.

But I do hope that this experience will encourage him to be less pompous in future.

Chapter 5

'Calm down, man,' said Dick Jackson. 'Your face is redder than yon James Galley's when he heard Maudlin Seam was flooded and couldn't be worked after he'd rented it for three year from Mister Martin. He dropped down dead of an apoplexy brought on by his fury. And that's what'll happen to you.'

'Calm down? Them two treat us like dirt under their feet and I've to calm down?'

'They're gentry, man. They've been treating you like that all the days of your life. Did you think being constable would change things?'

'Divven't call Maggie Laws Maggie, for isn't she better than you?'

Jackson laughed. 'There's a few round here called her sweeter names than that. We might have, too, if we'd been a bit younger.'

'And I haven't to say that Susannah Ward is a young woman, or a show-off. Or that she might scream if she saw a murdered woman.'

'Jeffrey, man. Drink your tea and shut up.'

'And nor is it right for the likes of me to have a watch.'

'Well, I manage without one.'

'I saved a year for this watch.' He took it from his pocket and gazed fondly at it. 'And I'll tell you something else. That overseer is sweet on young Kate Greener.'

'She's a bonny lass.'

'Kate Greener this and Kate Greener that. The man cannot stop saying her name.'

'Has he done her, do you think?'

'A man doesn't keep going on about a lass after he's had a ride of her. Dreaming, man. He's *dreaming* about doing her.'

'You cannot blame him for that. By God, there's something about that one.'

'There is an' all. If I was twenty year younger...'

'You'd still be too old. And so is Blakiston, the dirty bugger.'

'Get away, man. There's no more than seven or eight year between them. Thomas Urwin was nigh on fifty when he wed Isabella Boosty, and her not turned eighteen. He *was* a mucky devil, mind. And she only married him so he wouldn't have her father put away for debt. She'll have thought he'd be dead in a year.'

'Six month. She was a canny lass, Isabella.'

'And look what happened. Another twenty year he lived, and a smile on his face every day of it. She bore him six children. No, man. Blakiston is not too old for Kate Greener. He's too well born, but. That'll be what holds him back. He'll be one of them thinks you have to marry a girl to enjoy her and his family won't let him. And now he wants me to search New Hope Farm to see if Maggie Laws's killer left any traces. I said Susannah Ward would have cleaned the place too well and he said did I think she was covering her own tracks? The man's not right in the head.' He rubbed his chin. 'This is good tea.'

'It *is* good tea. And all the better for not having a penny paid on it to the Revenue. It came by sea from the Low Countries to the smugglers in Robin Hoods Bay, and from there to here. Has Job King talked to you?'

'About what?'

'He has not, then. We should have done what he did twenty year ago and gone to America. We could be as rich as he is.'

'If we were, I'd not have come back and rented Gaskell Lodge. What does he want here? He has no family left.'

'To show people what he's made of himself; that's what he wants. He had no more than us when he left Ryton and now he's hired me to work in his fields. He needs another man and I told him to ask you. He said he would.'

'Ay, well, mebbes he tried. I've been all over the place with this killing.'

'He's paying me more than I ever earned. From anyone. He'll pay you the same.'

At Chopwell Garth, Florrie brought the family together to discuss the disaster that had struck the Laws family. Tom said Joseph was free to stay as long as he liked.

'I'm a farmer,' said Joseph. 'I have to be on my farm, and in my fields. You know that. I should be there now. Who will look after my cattle? Susannah Ward? And we are half way through August and the men are due in a few days for the wheat harvest.'

'Ned is there,' said Tom. 'Your beasts are as safe as they would be if you were looking after them yourself.'

'Mebbes. Still, I must return.'

'Joseph,' said Florrie. 'You have suffered the most terrible shock. To come home and find your wife...you must take more time to recover.'

'Give me a dish of tea and a bite to eat, Florrie, and I'll be off. You'll be needing Ned here yourself, and I must be where I belong.'

'You'll leave Samuel with us, at least?'

'No, man. The poor bairn has lost his mother. Is he to lose his father, too?'

Lizzie said, 'If you won't leave the child here, Kate must come with you to look after him.'

Kate stepped forward from her place by the wall. 'Me?'

'Who else? Would you leave your brother-in-law to be a mother as well as a father?'

'He has Susannah Ward.'

'She's not family. And she'll be off some day soon, to marry Jemmy Rayne and have his bairns.'

Joseph said, 'You can help me choose papers for the hall and the back parlour, Kate. Margaret had them sent from James Wheeley in London, but she never got the chance...' He broke off, as though choked with emotion.

The room fell silent. Four pairs of eyes stared at Joseph. Then Kate said, 'Choosing papers is a wife's job. I'm not coming to New Hope to be your wife, Joseph Laws.'

'Of course not. I did not mean...I meant only...'

'It is a woman's place to choose wallpaper,' said Florrie. 'Everyone knows that. We'd live in a strange looking world if we let men decide what to put on the walls.'

Kate stepped forward, close to Joseph. 'I'll come for two weeks,' she said. 'Four at the most. While you make other arrangements. But don't think I'm coming to take Margaret's place, because I'm not. And don't think I'll stay, because I won't. And you'd better make sure there's a lock on my bedroom door, and that I have the only key.'

Those words cast a coldness that would not lift, and Joseph made haste to finish his tea and leave. When he had gone, he left behind four subdued people.

'His wife is dead,' said Lizzie, 'and he wants to talk about wallpaper. You have a strange brother, Tom.'

'He's deranged, man,' said Florrie. 'Grief has turned his head.'

'It's turned a long way if he thinks he's marrying me,' said Kate.

Tom said, 'Wallpaper! Was that his idea, do you think?'

'Nay, man,' said Lizzie. 'Margaret will have said what's wanted. Paper will be a good idea in that farmhouse. It has that many dark passages and little rooms where the sun never shines. Like this one.'

'Eh? You're not thinking of paper in Chopwell Garth?'

'I wasn't,' said Lizzie. 'I am now. But I'll give you a while to get used to the idea before we discuss it again.'

Chapter 6

That evening, Tom had business at Holy Cross Church and it was business that he hated. The Poor Law was administered for the benefit of the well-off who contributed the money that kept the poor afloat, but it was farmers – men of the middling sort who also contributed to the upkeep of paupers – who did the work. And Tom was now a farmer, and elected as an overseer of the poor.

The overseers met in the vestry every fourth Saturday with the rector in the chair and keeping the minutes. There was a reason for that; the rector would always be a man who could write and most of the farmers lacked that skill. It also gave the Reverend Claverley the chance to adjust decisions that failed to accord with the wishes of the Bishop of Durham, one of the three largest landowners. The most pressing business of the evening concerned a young woman on whom the rector fixed a cold eye. 'Ann Foreman. You have no husband, and yet you are pregnant.'

The young woman said nothing. Tom felt sympathy that he knew was out of place in an overseer of the poor. He was here to represent the moneyed classes, and not to sympathise with those who came before the overseers. He had no doubt that people who thought themselves his betters would see in Ann Foreman a threat to the very existence of ordered society. What he saw was a sad young woman in rags.

He knew how this was likely to end. She would bear a bastard child, and the death rate among bastards was high especially when – as in this case – the mother had no family to fall back on who might give her and her child a place to live. What the overseers were required to do was to find a man who could be forced to pay for the child's upkeep. If no such man could be identified, Ann Foreman would have to rely on the generosity of the parish. A generosity that did not stretch very far. He leaned forward. Gently, he said, 'Ann. You were walking out with James Golightly, were you not?'

The rector said, 'James Golightly is no use to us. The man is dead. Killed in a brawl in a Newcastle alehouse. For which no one has been arrested or is likely to be.'

'Nevertheless,' said Tom, 'if he is the father... Is that what happened, Ann? Are you pregnant by James Golightly? Did he promise to marry you before some Newcastle lout kicked him to death?'

As she nodded, the young woman before them burst into tears. 'He said he loved me. He said we would be together the rest of our lives.'

The rector's expression became even darker. 'Pah! Where would we be if every young woman in the land raised her skirts for every young man who said he loved her?' He leaned forward, glaring at Ann. 'Bankrupt. That's where we would be. You have behaved like a common harlot, and like a common harlot is how you will be treated.'

Tom's discomfort intensified. Rector Claverley had been in the crowd when Mary Stone had swung from the gibbet for the murder of her illegitimate child, conceived as part of her life as a prostitute – but Mary had only turned to prostitution when she was seduced by a man of the Blackett family while working in their Matfen Hall home as a maid and then turned out to fend for herself. Had the rector forgotten that? And had he forgotten also that it was the rector's previous curate, Martin Wale, who had been one of Mary Stone's most frequent customers? What did anyone imagine would happen to Ann Foreman now?

His thoughts were interrupted by a knock on the door. It opened to reveal the man Tom knew to be Job King's steward. The rector raised his eyebrows in a mute question as to why the meeting was being interrupted.

'Sirs,' said the steward. He lowered his head the minimum possible amount in the rector's direction. 'Reverend. Mr King has sent me here. It is about the matter of the young woman there.' He inclined his head in the direction of Ann Foreman.

'Ann Foreman? Surely, Job King is not acknowledging...'

'No, Reverend Claverley, Mr King is not the father of the young woman's child. But he has heard the story, he knows no aid can come from the child's father, and he wishes to help her.'

'He will have to do that in any case,' said the rector. 'Those of sufficient standing in the parish bear the costs of bastards when no father appears who can be made to take his responsibility. And Job King is a landowner and one of those of sufficient standing.'

'Yes, Rector, but Mr King knows the extent of parish generosity. He knows how often it ends in the death of the child. He does not want that to happen to Ann Foreman's child, because Ann Foreman's father and he were boyhood friends before Mr King went to the colonies.'

Tom felt a great warmth enter his heart. The young woman and her child were to be rescued. Even the rector's countenance looked lighter as he asked, 'And what does Mr King propose?'

'He offers Ann Foreman employment as a maid. She will be paid the same as Mr King's other maids, and Mr King will bear the costs of her lying in and of the raising of her child and its education. All he asks of her in return is that she lies with no man in the future unless she has previously married him.'

Tom looked at the young woman. He thought she might be about to cry, but the tears would be tears of great happiness and not of grief. She had been saved when she could not have expected it. Tom had never spoken to Job King, but clearly he was a very good man.

Ann Foreman said, 'I accept! I promise!'

The rector turned his disapproving eyes on her. 'It is not for you to accept or decline. We shall accept or decline on your behalf.' He looked around at the other overseers as he said, 'And we do accept, do we not, gentlemen?'

Every face smiled and every head nodded. 'We do.'

Claverley turned again to the steward. 'We will expect Mr King to sign a bond committing himself to these promises until the child shall reach the age of twelve years.'

The steward nodded. 'Mr King understands that. He asked me to tell you that he would sign such a bond as soon as it is presented to him. '

'You may thank Mr King on behalf of the parish, and tell him that I shall draw up the bond myself. If he would care to call on me at the rectory between the hours of two and three tomorrow afternoon, I shall have it ready for his signature.' Then he turned back to Ann Foreman, his glance already darkening. 'You, young woman, are far luckier than you had any right to expect. You may go, and I suggest that on your way out you stop in the church and thank God from the depths of your sinful soul for the kindness with which He has dealt with you.'

The meeting ended soon afterwards, and Tom set out to walk home. It was a pleasant evening and he was buoyed by Job King's generosity. If only everyone in the parish who could afford to act with such kindness would do so.

When he got home, he told the others what had happened. Lizzie said, 'What a good man! I wonder what made him do it?'

Florrie said, 'He knows from his own experience what can happen to children who are thrown on the parish. And to their mothers, if it come to that.'

'I know nothing about him,' said Tom. 'Only that he once lived here and has now returned from the colonies, a rich man.'

'I remember him leaving. I must have been twelve years old, because it was later that year that I went into service at the Mill. Job King was the same age. I know that, because Job and I were baptised in the same week and we were baptised in a hurry because there was a heating sickness. It was killing people, and it killed children most of all. They did not want Job and me to die without baptism, but nor did they want us in the church and so the rector of the time came to our cottages. They thought Job and I would die, but we both lived – it was Job's mother and father who died.'

'Did the parish pay to send him to the colonies?' asked Lizzie.

'Not they. The overseers put him and his older brothers and sisters into the family of a farmer. My memory is not what it was and I cannot now remember which farmer.'

'In this parish, though?'

'Yes, in this parish, because this is where his father was settled – the King family had been here for at least three generations from what my father told me when Job left – but not in this chapelry, which will be why I can't remember the farmer's name. The parish paid them, of course, but it will not have been much – it is never much – and they will often have been hungry.'

Tom smiled to think that his mother-in-law had travelled so little that she could not call to mind someone in her own parish but another chapelry.

'I see you grinning, Tom Laws. Not all of us are so fortunate that we can be away hobnobbing with people from the other side of the parish. For some of us, just the business of staying alive has meant being stuck in one place the whole of our lives.'

'I meant no offence, Florrie Greener. In any case, Job King did us overseers a very generous good deed.'

'Aye, he's a good man, right enough.'

'So how did he afford the journey?'

'I don't believe he did. I think he did what Kate and Lizzie's brother Joseph would have done had you not paid his fare to the Americas – he went as a bonded man, tied to work for another for his first five years there. Half of those who make that journey don't survive those first five years. Job King must have had God on his side.'

Job King went to the rectory at the appointed time to sign his bond. It might have occurred to him – indeed, it did occur to him – that, as a landowner and one who was doing an expensive favour for the parish, he might have expected that the rector would come to him. But what did it matter? He knew the rector to be someone likely to value his own status as an educated man and the second son of an aristocrat over that of someone, however rich, who had left this parish a pauper. Things like that mattered to the rector; Job cared nothing about them.

And for all that, Claverley's welcome was cordial enough. 'Mr King. Welcome. This is a generous act.'

'God has been good to me, Rector. It is my duty to pass on to others what I have received.'

Thomas shifted a little uneasily. Quoting one's duty to God was his job, and one he usually reserved only for his Sunday sermon in church. Nevertheless, there was no arguing with what the man had said. 'I have prepared the bond exactly as your butler indicated. But tell me: is it really appropriate to provide for the education of the bastard child of Ann Foreman and the late James Golightly?'

Job struggled not to laugh. His years in the colonies had accustomed him to religious feelings and statements that were, for the most part, genuine; his return had reacquainted him with English hypocrisy in matters of the church but he could not yet say that he was used to it. 'An educated man is less likely to become a charge on the parish when his own time comes.'

'I see your point. By paying now, you may save money later.'

The rector seemed impervious to the smile playing about Job's lips. 'In any case, here is the bond. And here is a pen. If you would like…' He stopped speaking, his face reddening. Job King's smile became broader.

'To make my mark? In fact, Rector, I learned to read and to write while I was in Virginia. Write well enough to sign my own name, at least.'

'My dear fellow, I did not mean…'

'Content yourself, Rector. I was a pauper here. Paupers could neither read nor write. As I have said, that is why I would like Ann Foreman's child to learn those skills. So that it – unlike me – will never be a pauper.'

'Commendable. But, tell me: Will you still hold that view if the child is a girl?'

'Even more so, for I have the highest regard for the intelligence of women and far too often I see it held back. Do you tell me that you are not educating your own daughter?'

'I… Well, certainly I… But she…'

This time, Job felt no compulsion to relieve Claverley from the hole he had dug for himself. "She is the daughter of a clergyman, while Ann Foreman is a person of no account." That was the thought in the rector's mind, even if he found it impossible to speak the words. Job signed the document before him and pushed it back across the desk for the rector to shake sand over the ink. He stood, as if to leave.

The rector, embarrassment still clear, said, 'My dear fellow. We have not yet entertained you to dinner at the rectory.'

That's true, thought Job, and the failure has caused me no discomfort at all. Nevertheless, an invitation was clearly coming, and he could not bring himself to be so rude as to reject it.

'I shall speak to Lady Isabella. I know she will share my wish to break bread with you.'

Job bowed his head in acknowledgement, and Thomas walked him to the front door.

Chapter 7

The following day was the twenty-sixth of August and a Sunday. The sun shone brilliantly and the morning was already warm at seven. Blakiston mounted Obsidian and set off towards the water meadows by the river at Stella. Near Hussey's Forge he met the animal doctor, Tobias Foster. Cordial nods were exchanged in the spirit of a warm Sunday morning.

'What brings you here, Foster?' asked Blakiston.

'Lord Widdrington's man wanted my opinion on a horse he has stabled on Shipley's Farm. Or he said he did.'

'You doubt it?'

'He asked my opinion and I gave it and I shall account to his Lordship for my trouble and see that he pays me. But there was nothing the matter with the horse and the man knew that. No, he is in a tizz over this canal that Wrightson's want, to connect Parsons Banks and Ryton Willows with their staithes near here.'

'My dear fellow, I will hear this story. Have you eaten breakfast?'

'I am on my way home now.'

'Come with me to the inn at Beggar's Bank. It is my pleasure to eat there by the river on a fine Sunday before church.'

Foster turned his horse in the direction Blakiston took and the two rode companionably side by side.

'You are not a church goer yourself, Foster?'

'No more by nature than I imagine you are. But I have no lord to defer to, and no appearances to keep up, and so I may please myself in the matter.'

When they were seated in the garden, surrounded by the sweet smell of roses and phlox, Blakiston ordered plates of cheese and ham. "Cut thickly, now. And this week's bread, if you please. We want nothing old or stale. And bring us two pots of small beer before you begin."

He turned to Foster. 'This canal. Will it ever come to pass, do you think?'

'Who can say? We have had canals mooted here before, and none built. The country around Stafford is so chopped and crossed by canals I wonder some portion of the land does not detach itself and float away into the Irish Sea, but in Durham and Northumberland we have not a one. But, you know, the route Wrightson's have in mind runs over land where Lord Widdrington has the freehold, and he wants the diggings to go forward to increase his rents. And so his man asks me to look at a horse that ails nothing, and all the time he is telling me how wonderful a canal would be for the people hereabouts.'

'Has he no friends at Parliament to advance his cause?'

'The Blacketts will not help a papist.'

'I am not from these parts, as you know.'

'The Widdringtons are wrapped up with many of our oldest families, and some not so old. The Brandlings and the Tempests among them. I believe Sir Edward Blackett tried to bribe you with a Tempest woman.'

'Are there no secrets? Grace Hodgson is a Tempest?'

'She is of that stock. This is fine ham. I wonder where he gets it?'

'He cures it himself. But Grace Hodgson is a cousin of Sir Edward. If she is a Tempest, and Tempests are married with Widdringtons, then the Blacketts have a family interest there. And still Sir Edward will not advance Widdrington's canal?'

'The last Lord Widdrington was a Jacobite. He took part in the Fifteen Rebellion and was sentenced to death. In fact, they did not hang him and he lived another thirty years, but all his estates were forfeit to the Crown except the ones hereabouts, because he had those through his wife. William Hodgson's daughter married Sir Thomas Tempest and *their* daughter married Widdrington and was this Widdrington's mother. Sir Edward Blackett rejects him as a son of Rome, or so he says, though we may suspect that his desire to limit the number of landowners of substance in the district may play a greater part than he would acknowledge.

'The Member of Parliament for Newcastle at the time of the uprising was Sir William Blackett and there are those who say that Widdrington expected his help in occupying the city. There are also those who believe that that was Sir William's original intention, and that he was swayed by Scarborough's arrival with more than twice the number of men Widdrington could put in the field. In any case, Widdrington was disappointed. There is no love lost between the two families even today. I must say, Blakiston, I admire your fortitude in rejecting Blackett's offer of Grace. I have always admired large-breasted women, and large-breasted women with a thousand a year are not so abundant as to be readily cast aside.'

'The figure Sir Edward mentioned was five hundred. Well, Widdrington must make his way as best he can. But I have wanted to see you, Foster, for I have a question and you may have the answer. When a man dies, he is limp. And then he goes stiff. And then he is limp again.'

'That is also true when a man is alive. Especially in the presence of such as Grace Hodgson. But you speak of the effects of rigor mortis.'

'Do I? Well, what I wish to know is, how long does it take for the first limpness to go? And, after that, how long before it returns?'

'I had heard of the death of Margaret Laws. You ask in connection with that?'

'I do.'

'Very well. The stiffness, or rigor as we call it, begins to show itself about three hours after death and is at its height after twelve. Then it begins to leave the body. But it is not completely absent until another three days have elapsed.'

'And it is the same for women as for men? Does it make a difference if the woman was expecting?'

'Do you tell me Maggie Laws was with child? Is the father known?'

'Is the father...for the love of God, Foster, you are speaking of a married woman.'

'Ah, yes. So I am. What can I have been thinking of?'

'Look here, Foster. Is there something I should know about the dead woman? Rector Claverley felt the constable spoke slightingly of her. Or at least that he lacked respect. And now you ask such a question. Was she a wanton? Is this something all know but the Rector and I?'

'I am sure she was no more than a red-blooded woman.'

'So there *was* something...'

'I shall say no more, Blakiston. As you have reminded me, she was married, and to a man raising himself into the middling sort. I regret any untoward allusion. The common kind will snigger and hint, and you and I should pay no heed.'

'But...'

'There are no buts. I must be about my business, and you will have your own to attend to. Thank you for my breakfast. I must bid you good day.'

Blakiston sat a little longer in the garden of this house for which he had great affection but where now he found a cloud over his enjoyment. The implication of Foster's offhand question was clear: that Margaret Laws had been no better than she should have been, that paternity of her child was open to doubt and that her husband must therefore come under suspicion for her death.

That meant that times became important: the time that Margaret Laws had been killed; the time that she had been discovered; the time that help had been sought. Blakiston realised with a start that he had not even established what time Joseph Laws had arrived home that morning, or how long afterwards it had been when he reached Chopwell Garth. He finished his pot of ale, pushed the last of his bread and ham into his mouth, left coins on the table and hurried outside to his horse.

As Tobias Foster had hinted, Blakiston went to church because he had to. Lord Ravenshead did not much mind what his employees actually believed, so long as they kept to the expected forms of Church of England devotion. His Lordship had his own chapel and his own chaplain and so did not worship at Holy Cross Church in Ryton, but he would hear of anyone who was absent from Thomas's services and he would make his views known. Blakiston therefore rode to Ryton after breakfast, left Obsidian in his own stable and walked across the green to the church. He did not want to face Thomas but saw no way to avoid it.

He would have hurried away as soon as it was over, and indeed he stood and left the church as the last blessing was given and before the Rector could get outside to say goodbye to his parishioners, but Isabella had foreseen this manoeuvre and was there before him.

'Please wait,' she said.

'Lady Isabella...'

'Please, Mister Blakiston. My husband and I talked until late into the night. We wish you to come to dinner tonight.'

'But Lady...'

'I have told Rosina you will be there. She is preparing a special meal. And I know you cannot bring Kate while you are only engaged to be married. But when she is Mistress Blakiston, know that she will be as welcome a guest at the Rectory as you are. And I speak for the Rector as well as for me. He has been so angry with himself at having taken such a thoughtless position. I can tell you he has something very positive to say to you about reading your banns, which *he* will do, and marrying you to Kate, which *he* will also do.'

Blakiston was silent. Then he said, 'How can I possibly refuse?'

'Thank you, Mister Blakiston. I promise you my husband will be even more pleased than I am. And I am delighted.'

Next, Blakiston went home to mull over his next steps in looking for the killer of Margaret Laws and to give the people he wanted to speak to time to get home from church. Then he rode to Chopwell Garth, for Kate must hear the glad news of the Rector's change of heart, and the sooner the better.

'Joseph is not here, Mister Blakiston,' said Lizzie. 'He has returned to New Hope to see that all is well. Kate will join him there this afternoon.'

'Kate? For what purpose?'

'You have turned white, sir. I did not mean to startle you. May I bring you some water?'

'There is no need. Kate; what will she do at that farm?'

'She is to look after little Samuel, Sir. The bairn must have a mother.'

'And the bairn's father? Must he have a wife?'

Lizzie stared at Blakiston, but said nothing. The silence continued so long that he was obliged to break it himself. 'Mistress Laws, I have asked Kate to marry me and Kate has said yes. As you are aware. She does not want it to be public knowledge until she is ready to fix our wedding day and she will not do that till I have calmed her fears about the gentry and my family, but you know that we are to be husband and wife. I could understand your opposition when you thought my intentions dishonourable, but you are still opposed and I would know why.'

Lizzie sighed. 'Life is not so simple, sir. I cannot speak my mind. My husband depends on you for his living. You are gentry. I am but a common person. As is Kate.'

'Am I to be discussed while I am out of the room?'

Blakiston stepped back. 'Kate! I did not hear you enter. You are to leave Chopwell Garth?'

'No, sir, I am not to leave. I am to go to New Hope Farm, which is not a half hour from here by horse, though I have no such thing to take me there.'

'I had noticed the coach you arrived in was gone. You have told Mistress Wortley that we are to marry?'

'No, James, I have not. And you know why. I wrote her a note to say that I must stay for longer than I had expected, and that I did not feel I could keep the coach and coachman here, and that it might be best if she found a new lady's maid. But I shall stay at New Hope for not more than four weeks while Joseph Laws finds someone willing to be a mother to his son. I am not that person.'

Clicking her tongue in irritation, Lizzie walked out of the room.

'The matter of the horse is easily settled,' said Blakiston. 'I shall take you on mine, for I must go there in any case. I wish to speak to Joseph Laws.'

'I have my things to carry. I cannot ride on a horse with two bags.'

'I shall send a man to take whatever you wish. And to bring them back when your four weeks are done.'

Kate smiled. 'Thank you. What is it you wish to speak to Joseph about?'

'A question I may put also to you. I need to know at exactly what time he returned home on the morning his wife was killed, and at what time he arrived here.'

'I can answer for the last. He arrived here a moment after seven, for the clock you see on that wall and which is such a matter of pride to our Lizzie since it arrived but four weeks past had just finished chiming. I can tell you it is right for it agrees with the church clock, although in Lizzie's view it is the other way about. She was seeing to little Lulu's breakfast and Tom and Ned had been in the fields since five and were about to sit down for theirs. Tom remarked on the time.'

'His exact words?'

'He looked at the clock and said, "Great God, Joe man hinny, just seven and you here already? Is summat up?"'

Blakiston laughed out loud. 'You are a good witness. And then Joseph Laws told you his wife was dead?'

'James, I must be on my way to New Hope. If you are to take me, can we talk about this on the way?'

Chapter 8

He had been in church with the others, for why should he not? He had a right to worship there. At least as much right as those hypocrites, which indeed appear beautiful outward, but are within full of dead men's bones, and of all uncleanness. Give alms of such things as ye have; and, behold, all things are clean unto you.

But you knew better, did you not? All four of you. Four of you killed four of mine. Or let them die, which comes to the same thing.

And four of you will have someone die in your turn. For we know him that hath said, Vengeance belongeth unto me, I will recompense, saith the Lord. And again, The Lord shall judge his people.

He had heard the man after church, talking to the Rector, saying that God had taken his son and his son's wife but spared his grandson. He thought that, did he? Well, he would learn soon enough that God was not done with him yet.

It was not the first time Blakiston had ridden behind Kate, but it was the first time since he had asked her to marry him and she had said yes. There was a difference now in the way he felt. Tension and worry were gone. Now, when he was in this young woman's company, he was calm.

Now, when he put his arms round her waist to keep her safe, when his nose drifted into the curls at the base of her hair and his lips gently nuzzled the back of her neck, he knew that this was how life was meant to be. This was what love was. This was why there were women as well as men.

'I am going to dinner at the Rectory tonight,' he murmured, confident that she would understand his meaning.

'You are? As a friend?'

'As a friend.'

'Oh, I'm glad.'

'Be gladder. The Rector will call our banns, and the Rector will marry us. Just as soon as you say the word.'

'Oh, James! What ever changed his mind?'

'He has the love of a good woman himself. How could he go on denying me the same joy?'

'It's Lady Isabella. Isn't it? She has spoken to him.'

Gently, he squeezed her waist between his arms. 'I said, in case you were not paying attention, the Rector will call our banns just as soon as you say the word.'

'Oh, James! But what about your sister?'

'My darling love, Hannah is not going to change her mind, and so you must put her out of yours. Tell me I can have the banns called.'

Kate turned her face towards him. 'Do it. Do it next Sunday.'

They kissed, a long lingering kiss that only ended when Obsidian threatened to ride them into a wall. They rode on for a while, cheek resting against cheek. 'I never believed I could be this happy,' said Blakiston.

Kate laughed. 'Think of the amazement on Sunday when our banns are called. Oh, James, please let us keep it a secret until then, just so that I can see people's faces.'

'Whatever you like, my dearest girl.'

'I shall sit at the back, so that I can see everyone when they hear the news.'

Blakiston smiled. 'You shall do so for the last time, in that case. After this Sunday, when the banns have been read and our secret is known, I shall expect you to join me in my own pew.'

They rode in companionable silence. Then Kate said, 'We are nearly there, my sweet. There were questions you wanted to ask?'

'Margaret Laws,' said Blakiston. 'What can you tell me about her?'

Kate shrugged. 'She was Joseph's wife. Really, I never liked her.'

'Because?'

'Oh. I don't think there was anything particularly...she was stuck up, I suppose. You know it was only in April that she and Joseph wed. Her husband had died, and she had a son for whom she needed a father. Her own father has quite a big farm on the Bishop's estate. Joseph was another farmer, so she married him. I don't believe she ever loved him. Nor do I think she thought much of the rest of us. Tom was a second son who should have been a labourer. Lizzie should have been skivvying for the likes of her instead of running her own farmhouse. And as for me...well, she never spoke to me if she could help it.'

'I heard...someone said something to me...there was a suggestion...'

'That Margaret was no better than she should have been. Yes, people say that.'

'With reason?'

'James, Margaret was a farmer's wife. She lived in a farmhouse. Her husband lived there too, and so did Susannah Ward. Others would have been in and out, for while Tom has changed to paying day labourers when he needs them, Joe still sticks to the old way of hiring his farm workers for the year. Apart from at harvest time, of course. Never mind whether Margaret might have wanted to betray Joe. What time did she have? What opportunity?'

'I had forgotten that Joe hires workers at the fair. Why was he in such a hurry to get back if he has someone to look after his livestock?'

'He hired but the one man, though his father always had three, even when Tom was there. Tom thinks he drove the man too hard. And he ended his employment a few weeks back.'

'I did not know that.'

'You are the overseer. Should he not have told you?'

'I have had other things on my mind.'

'That added to the rumours, for there were those who said the man was sacked because he had dealings with Margaret he should not have had.'

'Good God. Was this true?'

'You would have to ask Joseph. Or the hired man, of course. Emmett Batey is his name. But a past like Margaret's will make people talk even more than already they do.'

'Her past?'

'I do not know the whole story; only that Samuel was her son but not the son of her first husband. And Tom's mother did not want his brother to marry her because she feared there would be more children and Joseph would not be the father of those. Joseph may have thought she was right.'

'Then why did he marry her?'

'It was not for love as your marriage to me will be, you may be sure of that.' She pressed her lips against his cheek. 'In fact, you were to blame.'

'Me?'

'In a way. Joseph was the oldest son and should have had New Hope Farm when his father died...'

'As he did.'

'...but would he have had it without a wife? You see! Your face gives you away. You do not like a farmer to be unmarried.'

'It is true. I do not.'

'And so Joseph took the wife who was available, not to have a wife but to keep a farm. In any case, Ned had to go there to see that all was well while Joseph was at the Garth. And now Ned will be free to return home to help Tom, and I have told Joseph that I will stay at New Hope for four weeks and no more.' She turned again to look at Blakiston, her eyes shining, her hands waving. 'Which, if our banns are to be called on Sunday, is all I will be able to do, because after three weeks we will be free to wed. Oh, James! Is your brother on shore? Will he be able to be your groom's man?'

'I shall write to him today and ask him.'

'Oh, I do hope so. James, I want to have little Jameses.'

'And little Kates?'

'Your children, James. I want to have your children.'

'Our children.'

'Oh, James. You are the most wonderful man. I should like to squeeze you to pieces. I should like to eat you all up.'

Blakiston hugged her. Then he said, 'There is one thing I do not understand.'

'Why do I have to go to New Hope Farm? Why did Joseph not simply leave little Samuel at the Garth?'

'Exactly. Yes.'

'Because he knew, if he insisted on taking the bairn with him, Lizzie or our Mam would send me with them, to look after the child.' Her eyes were solemn. 'He hoped he would get to keep me, James. Lizzie hoped so, too. She feels I would be better suited with a man of my own sort.'

'The blackguard. I should horsewhip him.'

Kate laughed. 'Please don't, James. For my sake.'

Perhaps Blakiston might have behaved differently if he had not heard what he had, and had Joseph's reaction to their arrival been other than it was. It seemed to Blakiston that the look Joseph cast on Kate was nakedly lascivious, which Blakiston was never going to appreciate. And then the farmer tried to brush him off.

'Mister Blakiston,' said Joseph. 'I have no time to talk. I must be out on my land.'

'Kate,' said Blakiston. 'Will you please take charge of Samuel? And take him for a walk, for your brother in law seems distracted by your presence. And you, Susannah Ward, find something in another room to occupy yourself.'

When the two women had left, he addressed Joseph. 'You must be out on your land. That is an interesting choice of words, for you have no land. It is not your land, it is Lord Ravenshead's land, and I am Lord Ravenshead's overseer and you would do well to remember that. You no longer have a wife, Laws, and it is my opinion that a farmer with a baby son and no wife will struggle to manage Lord Ravenshead's land as I would have it managed. Perhaps I may end your tenancy of this farm. Perhaps I may do so today.'

'But Master...'

'Ah! Master! You remember who you are speaking to. I have some questions I wish to ask you, Laws, and I expect you to answer them. Inspecting what you choose to call your land can wait until I am satisfied. Is that clear?'

'Yes, Master.'

'I wish to understand what happened yesterday morning. I will hear your account from the beginning. Starting with why you were not here when your wife was done to death.'

'Sir, I had gone to Carlisle.'

'For what purpose?'

'I was summoned there. On a fool's errand.'

'I think you had better explain.'

'Master, I received a letter. My wife could read and she read it to me. It said I must be in Carlisle yesterday, that I must present myself at the Bull Hotel near the Castle walls, that I must arrive there no earlier than eight o' the evening and no later than nine, and that I would be given something that would make me a rich man.'

'And you travelled sixty miles on no better word than that?'

'I did not want to go. But my wife said if I did not she would be furious with me. She called me an obstinate fool and said I was spurning the chance to be a rich man and make her a rich man's wife.'

'Sometimes a wife's opinion is best ignored.'

'That is easy for you to say, Master, for you are not married.'

'In any case, you went. This letter. Who did your wife say it was from? In fact, where is the letter now?'

'She said it was from Lord Worrall. Who I confess I never heard of. The letter will be somewhere hereabouts. She did not want me to take it with me to Carlisle but I insisted. I had it in mind to show it to the people at The Bull.'

'And did you?'

'There is no Bull, Master. Carlisle is a meagre little place of few people and all of them poor. They have five inns but none is called The Bull. I was sent there for no reason. Perhaps someone's idea of a jest.'

'I see. This letter – how did it arrive?'

'I suppose the post boy brought it.'

'You suppose? You did not see him?'

'I would have been in my...in the fields. Margaret showed me the letter when I came in at midday for dinner. She also read it to me for she has that skill and I have not.'

'Why you did not return from Carlisle till after sun-up?'

'Master, the road is not good to travel at night. There are footpads and highwaymen and the road itself is poor.'

'Susannah Ward, have I given you leave to come into this room?'

'Sir, I have my work to do.'

'Do it elsewhere.'

The maid looked at him with anger in her eyes, but went. 'She merely wanted to hear what you have to say,' he said to Joseph. 'Doubt not it would have been all over the parish by nightfall. Let us return to your wife's death. What time was it when you reached home after you had been wherever you had been?'

'Sir, it was about fifteen minutes after six of the clock.'

'You arrived alone? You saw no sign of Susannah Ward?'

'No, Master.'

'What *did* you see?'

Joseph's eyes filled with tears. 'Sir, I saw Margaret, dead.'

'And what did you do?'

'Sir, I ran to my horse and rode to Chopwell Garth.'

'You left your son here?'

'Yes, Master.'

'Alone?'

'Yes, Master.'

'Why?'

'Master?'

'Your son is scarce two years old. I am no father, but I know that a child of that age is unable to care for himself, so why, knowing that he was alone, did you leave him here?'

'I do not know.'

'You do not know. Your story does not hang together, man. Kate is here because you insisted your son must be with you, though in fact he is not your son, and not be left in the care of three women at Chopwell Garth; and yet you were content to leave him on his own with a murderer somewhere about. Before you set off for your brother's farm, did you inspect your wife?'

'Inspect, Master?'

'How closely did you look at her? You made sure she was dead? Did you remove any of her clothing?'

'No, Master.'

'So you did not know that your wife had been beaten as well as strangled?'

'I...no, sir.'

'Really. Let me tell you something about bruises, Laws. For I have seen these bruises, and they were most interesting. When a bruise is new, it is red. After two or three days, it becomes purple. A few more days and it turns yellow. After two or three weeks, it disappears.'

'Is that so, Master?'

'It is. And what was interesting about your wife's bruises is that some were purple and some were yellow. But none was red.'

Joseph Laws stared at the ground in silence.

'What that means, Laws, is that your wife was not beaten at the time she was killed. She had been beaten before. And more than once, for some of her bruises were older than others.'

Still Joseph said nothing.

'Tell me about your relations with your wife.'

'Master?'

'Were they normal? Did you *have* relations with her?'

'*Yes*, sir.'

'And did she keep her clothes on at the time?'

'No, sir.'

'So you saw her naked?'

'Yes, sir.'

'Then you will have seen the bruises.'

'She was a clumsy woman, Master. For ever walking into things. She would bang her body on the furniture.'

'Would she, indeed. How long have you known that your wife was expecting a child?'

'Why, almost since she fell for it. She told me as soon as she knew.'

'And had you any reason to doubt that the child was yours?'

The attack came so suddenly and with such force that Blakiston was unable to avoid it. Joseph Laws seized the black iron pot from a hook over the empty fire and smashed it with all his strength into the overseer's knee. As Blakiston staggered, the pot was swung again, this time at his head. A direct hit, Blakiston would say later, would have killed him. The glancing blow Laws actually scored merely laid him out on the floor, unconscious.

Chapter 9

When Blakiston came to, he was lying on the floor with Kate hovering over him. Jeffrey Drabble stood in the background, turning his round hat in his hand. Of Susannah Ward there was no sign.

Blakiston rolled onto his side and tried to stand. 'Quick,' said Kate. 'Help him.'

The constable came forward. Dropping his hat on the floor, he put his hand under Blakiston's arm. 'Begging your pardon, sir,' he murmured as he did his best to bring him to the vertical.

'We were going to lift you onto the settle,' said Kate. 'But it is so narrow and you thrashed around so much I was afraid you would fall off.'

'I shall sit there now,' said Blakiston. He rested his head in both hands. 'Thank you, Drabble. The schoolmaster always said I had a hard head. Though I do not think this was what he had in mind. Now you had better tell me what happened. Where is Susannah Ward? Did Joseph Laws get away? And how did you get here, Constable?'

'Susannah went for him,' said Kate. 'I told her to run, and to tell Jeffrey Drabble to run here. I expect she is making her way home more slowly.'

'But that means that you were here alone, while I could not have protected you. Where is the baby?'

'He is sleeping. And I did not believe Joseph Laws would come near, once he had run off like that.'

'Well, at any rate you can no longer stay here to take care of Samuel while that madman is running around. I think we know now who murdered his wife. You will have to take the boy back to Chopwell Garth. But someone must remain. You, Drabble. I wish you to guard this house and sleep here each night.'

'How long for, Master?'

'Until I tell you to stop. Don't worry about looking for Laws. He'd probably kill you, too. We'll get the militia to find him.'

'But, Master, I must work. If I don't work, I won't have money to eat.'

'You will be working. You will work here. And the Estate will pay you.'

'Oh. Thank you, Master. Master...'

'What is it now?'

'Sir, if I am to stay here at nights, can I ask Dick Jackson to stay here with me?'

Blakiston's eyes glittered. 'Ah, yes. Dick Jackson. The man who went to war with Daniel Dobson and came home alone, but carrying Dobson's money and his leather jerkin. Your cousin Dick Jackson. Dick Jackson of the mysterious past. Are you ready to tell me his secret?'

'Secret, Master?'

'His secret. I know there is one, Drabble, and I know that you know what it is. Why do you want him to stay here?'

At that point, the door opened and Susannah Ward limped into the kitchen.

'Perhaps we should ask the maid,' said Blakiston. 'She will be here too, I suppose? Susannah Ward, you are tired from your exertions?'

'It is a long way, Master. I see you are recovered from your blow. What is it that you need to ask me?'

'Joseph Laws killed his wife. I do not think we can be in any doubt about that now. He had been beating her for some time, and then he killed her. The picture is clear enough. He was willing to leave the boy here alone because it was never his boy. I suspect he did not believe the child she carried was his, either. And that will be why she died. Until he is captured we must take care. And so I have asked the constable to work here by day, and sleep here at night, and he has asked for Dick Jackson to work and stay here with him. I take it you raise no objection?'

'Dick will not work here, Master,' said Drabble, 'for he is already hired as a day labourer by Job King. He would be here only at night.'

'I see. You want more company in the evenings than Susannah Ward can provide. We would not pay Jackson to spend only his nights here.'

'No, sir. But he could have his supper here? And his breakfast?'

'I suppose he could. Well, Susannah Ward? What do you say to this?'

'Where will Samuel be, Master?'

'I have not thought about that. But not here.'

'I will take him to Chopwell Garth,' said Kate. 'He belongs to our family. We will look after him.'

'You won't give him to the overseers of the poor?'

Blakiston said, 'How could they do that? What is the first thing the overseers want to know when someone goes to them for help? They ask if there are relatives with money. The parish will not pay if someone else can.'

'And Tom is an overseer now,' said Kate. 'So he will know these things. Why do you look like that when I say Tom is become an overseer?'

'I don't look like anything,' said Susannah.

'Yes you do. When you said don't give Samuel to the overseers you looked something fierce. And when I said Tom was an overseer now, I thought you were going to spit.'

'You are a farmer's sister. You never had any trouble with the Poor Law. You have no idea what it's like.'

'I am not a farmer's sister. I am a farm labourer's daughter. When my father was dying, the overseers came. Of course.'

'Enjoy it, did you?'

'It was horrible. But it is over.'

'For some of us it is never over.'

'Enough,' said Blakiston. He stood, wincing when his damaged knee took the weight. 'I have asked you a question, Susannah Ward. Do you have any objection to Dick Jackson staying here with Jeffrey Drabble?'

'But, Master, if there is no child to look after and no family, there is no need for a maid. I had better look for a new position.'

'Not yet,' said Blakiston, 'for we need someone to carry out Margaret Laws's work. You must feed the pigs and the chickens, and you must milk the cows. Look at the constable's hands. Would you like something as rough as that on your own udders?'

She placed her hands on her hips, her mouth screwing itself up to reply.

'Then why should you think a cow will feel differently?' Blakiston went on before she could get the words out. 'And, if the two of them are to spend their nights here, someone will have to prepare breakfast and supper for them.'

'I am to be a maid for labourers now!'

'You have been so before, for there have been hired men at this farm most of the time you worked here. And when the harvest begins there will be the allowances to prepare for the men who come to do the work. But enough. I have things to do. Kate, bring the child and let us get the two of you on my horse. Oh – and, Drabble. Joseph Laws told me that the post boy came yesterday morning with a letter. I should like you to seek him out for me and ask him if that is true.'

'It is,' said Susannah Ward.

'What?'

'It is true. I was here. The post boy came. He brought a letter.'

'Well, Drabble, you will speak to the post boy and confirm that that is so.'

Susannah Ward looked as though she would speak, and as if what she said would be venomous, but she saw the expression on Blakiston's face and kept her peace.

When they reached Chopwell Garth, Blakiston declined the offer of roast beef with the rest of the family but accepted bread and cheese and a dish of tea. 'I am due at the Rectory tonight,' he explained, 'and there will be too much to eat already, without being too full to sit down to the table in the first place. You are sombre, Tom.'

'Master, I can not believe that my brother is a murderer.'

'If he is not, he was foolish to run.'

'Will you raise a hue and cry?'

'We are too busy to have men taken out of the fields to search for him. Especially as he took a fresh horse and could be many miles away. The Rector is a Justice of the Peace and I shall ask him to issue a warrant for Joseph's arrest. To do less would be negligent.'

'Will you send word to Carlisle?'

'Why should I do that?'

'Sir, if that is where he was when Margaret died...'

'You are not listening to me, Tom. Your brother strangled his wife. That means that he was at home when she died. You cannot strangle someone at a distance. This whole story of being in Carlisle, and coming home to find his wife dead on the floor, is fabrication. What I am concerned about now is who to send as the new tenant at New Hope.'

'But there are so many men thrown off the land.'

'I did not mean I could think of no-one. I can think of too many. But I shall discuss that with His Lordship when we meet tomorrow. And now I must be off.'

Blakiston was prepared for awkwardness when he entered the Rector's study that evening. There was none. Thomas welcomed him at the front door with a smile and a handshake so warm that he had for a moment the appalling fear that a man might be about to hug him for the first time since he had been a toddling boy in frocks, but nothing so dreadfully un-English happened. Instead, Thomas led the way into his den and poured a large glass of Madeira wine for each of them.

'James,' he said. 'I have behaved like the most utter fool. I beg your forgiveness.'

'Let us speak of it no more. I have already forgotten it.'

'I wish to call your banns on Sunday. And I want you to know that I look forward to welcoming your bride into my home.'

'It will give me the greatest possible pleasure to bring her here. And now, may we speak of other things? For I confess I wish us to put that whole unhappy time behind us. You are a Justice of the

Peace. Will you please issue a warrant for the arrest of Joseph Laws?'

'Joseph Laws? I shall, of course, but my dear fellow, you must tell me the story.'

And Blakiston did, and Thomas issued the warrant, and then they went in to dinner with Lady Isabella. The soup was mushroom, there was trout, a pot roast of beef and a roast chicken, after which Isabella ate candied fruit while the Rector shared his inevitable cheese with Blakiston. Three bottles of claret were consumed by the two men. The conversation touched briefly on the murder of Margaret Laws but moved swiftly on to a topic much closer to Isabella's heart when Blakiston asked how the new additions to the rectory were faring.

'Alice and Miles,' said Isabella. 'You know, my husband did not want to take these poor little ones into our home.'

Thomas made no attempt to dispute this remark.

'And I think he believed that I felt as I did only because I had lost the child I was carrying. And perhaps that was so. But those children have brought laughter into this house, and even Thomas has been seen to smile. Though not our new curate.'

'He does not like children?'

'He does not approve of these. Do you know what he said? "And I will not have mercy upon her children; for they be the children of whoredoms."'

'You are familiar with the Book of Hosea, James?' asked the Rector.

Blakiston shook his head.

'God told Hosea to marry a harlot.'

'Good Lord.'

'Which, of course, Mary Stone was, and Mary was the mother of Alice and Miles. In Hosea's case, the harlot's name was Gomer, and she bore Hosea a son. His name in English was God Sows. Then she bore him a daughter, and they named her Unloved, and then another son, who was probably not Hosea's.'

'Thomas, my dear friend. Is there a point to all this?'

'There is, James, and it is that God loves Israel as a man loves his wife, but that Israel turned away from God, and you cannot do that without punishment. God is just, but He is exacting.'

'Yes, yes,' said Lady Isabella. 'Be that as it may, Mister Fawcett had better moderate his language when he speaks of those dear to me or he, too, might find himself facing a wrathful countenance. He certainly will not find himself invited to sit at this table.'

'So, Thomas,' said Blakiston. 'You have softened towards Mary Stone's children?'

'The Poor Law shall not trample them as most orphans are trampled. They are not to be brother and sister to our daughter Catherine, but they will live here until they are old enough to look after themselves. They will learn to read and write and do their sums. Job King gave me an excellent lesson on that subject only yesterday. And they shall know what it is to eat a nourishing meal every day.'

'And God will bless you for it, husband,' said Isabella. 'And now I shall leave you both to your wine. Mister Blakiston, it has been such a pleasure to see you again at our table. And next Sunday, we shall invite Mistress Spence and Job King to join us. Job King is clearly a good man, however mean his origins, and in Mistress Spence we have a woman of common sense who will give us good conversation.'

Blakiston stood. 'The pleasure has been mine, Lady Isabella.' Blakiston had never done anything so dreadfully foreign as to kiss a lady's hand, but he bowed his head.

But Isabella had no sooner left the room than she was back. 'You said that you had issued a warrant for the arrest of Joseph Laws, husband?'

'I have, not three hours ago.'

'Would that all of your wishes could be answered so quickly. The servants are full of the news. Joseph Laws was arrested this evening in Darlington. Jeffrey Drabble is on his way there now with three dragoons, to bring him home to face justice.'

Chapter 10

Next morning, Blakiston rode to the Durham County Gaol in Saddler Street where Joseph Laws was held. As usual when he made this journey he took care that his pistols were loaded and ready to hand, for the road past Dunston Banks where the bridge took it over the River Team before he could join the main road south was a notorious hiding place for footpads. The journey, however, passed without incident.

Blakiston knew the jail from the time when Mary Stone and Martin Wale had been taken from there to be hanged. He had felt then that the very stones were blackened by three and a half centuries of grief and degradation. The place had not improved. Of course, treating prisoners well would cost money and those who had money might think it better spent on more deserving causes. Nevertheless, pity engulfed Blakiston when the gaoler brought the prisoner into the small room where the overseer waited, for Joseph bore the marks of a fight. 'Did you resist the dragoons, Laws?'

'I am not such a fool.' He touched the cuts around his blackened eye below which blood had dried in a knot that, taken with the jagged tears in his shirt, made him look like a captured pirate.

'This was done here, by scoundrels wanting money.'

'When did you eat last?'

'Yesterday morning, at Chopwell Garth before I returned home. I have been left with no means of paying for food.'

Blakiston called the gaoler and gave him ten shillings. 'One of these shillings is for you, to take care of the prisoner and see no harm befalls him. Send out for bread and cheese and a bumper of small beer. I want to see him properly fed every day, morning and night, and I shall require an accounting of the nine shillings each time I come. Before you feed him, bring a bowl of water, soap and a cloth.'

'Soap! There's no soap here, Overseer.'

'Then buy some. And reserve it for this prisoner alone. So, Laws,' he said when the gaoler had left on his errands, 'let us have a clean breast of it. Why did you kill your wife?'

'Sir, I did not.'

'Don't be a fool, man. What other reason could you have had for attacking me?'

But Joseph was not going to answer, and after he had made sure that the gaoler had obeyed his instructions, and Joseph was washed and breakfasted, Blakiston rode away no wiser than when he had arrived.

When he reached Ryton, Blakiston went first to New Hope Farm where he found Jeffrey Drabble in the fields. 'When you arrested Joseph Laws last night, did he give you any trouble?'

'Trouble? No, Master.'

'He went with you without a struggle?'

'Quiet as a lamb, Master.'

'Did he say anything on the journey?'

'Yes, Master.'

When no more words came, Blakiston stared at the man. Was it possible that this innocent face hid a rebellious nature? Worse, was he being mocked? 'Well? Out with it.'

'Sir, he said he had not killed his wife. He said she deserved to die but he had not killed her.'

'Deserved to die? Did he say why?'

'No, Master. But I should think…'

'Yes? What should you think?'

'Master, the Rector did not like it when I…'

'The Rector is not here to listen to you, Drabble. I am, and I should like to know what it is that you should think.'

'Yes, Master. Well, Master, you know that Maggie Laws…I am sorry, I am to say Mistress Margaret…you know that she was with child.'

'I do know that, Drabble. Yes.'

'Well, Sir, Joseph Laws may wonder whether the child she was to have was his.'

'Ah. Again this comes up. Why? Why are people so sure that Margaret Laws was carrying another man's child?'

'Sir. Margaret Laws was Walter Maughan's daughter. His second daughter. Walter Maughan is a farmer on the Bishop's land and he has three sons as well as Margaret and her sister. George is the eldest boy and he will take over the farm when his father is too old. Margaret was a flighty girl, Master. When she was just sixteen and not married she fell for a bairn.'

'She married the father? But that could not have been the son she brought Joseph, for the boy is too young.'

'She did not marry the father because she never said who he was.'

'But she would have been questioned?'

'No, Master. Walter Maughan was a church warden and an overseer of the poor and he would not see his own daughter brought before the others so he gave his bond that her child would never be a charge on the parish. There were those that smiled, for Walter is no friend to the poor. He guards parish money as his own. But the babe was stillborn and so his bond was not needed. Then when Margaret was twenty-two she fell again and this time Walter married her off to Ezekiel

Patterson who farmed north of the Tyne, in Chollerford.'

'Was he the father?'

'It was said he was. But it was also said that Walter give him five hundred pound to take his daughter and her bastard child off his hands.'

'Five hundred pounds? A fortune. Do you believe it?'

'Sir, these things always grow in the telling. But I do believe he bought his daughter a husband, and his grandson a father.'

'Perhaps I should ask him. Did you speak to the post boy?'

'Yes, sir. He delivered a letter to New Hope Farm the day before yesterday.'

'Delivered? Or did not deliver?'

'Delivered, sir. He did deliver it.'

'I see. I was not expecting that. I know it chimes with what Susannah Ward had to say, but still I did not expect it.'

'Beg pardon, sir, but could we say something about the work I am to do here?'

'It is harvest time and about to be busy. Let us meet tomorrow after breakfast at Chopwell Garth and we will discuss it together with Tom Laws.'

It was only as he rode to Chopwell Garth to tell Tom of this meeting that Blakiston wondered why

Walter Maughan had not come to Ryton when he heard his daughter was dead, and when he did he also wondered why he had not wondered such an obvious thing earlier. He asked Tom whether Maughan had been informed.

'Not by me, Master.'

''For goodness sake, Tom, I am soon to marry your sister-in-law. You cannot continue to call me Master. And now I see I have alarmed you. Did you always show so clearly on your face what was happening behind it?'

'But, sir, what should I call you if not Master or Sir?'

'Hmm. I see what you mean. What Kate will call me would not be right on your lips.' If he had meant to raise a smile with Tom, he was disappointed. 'You must call me nothing.'

'Nothing, Master.'

'Nothing. Not nothing, Master. So, when you said "Not by me, Master," you will in future say, "Not by me."'

'That will not be easy, sir.'

'That will not be easy.'

'I am sorry, sir. That will not be easy. I mean, I am sorry, that will not be easy.'

'Try. Practice makes all things possible. In any case, you did not send word to Walter Maughan that his daughter had been murdered.'

'I had no-one to send. And I did not think he would care.'

'His own daughter?'

'He had cut her from his life. He did not attend her wedding to Joseph.'

'Is that so? Well, I must seek him out and learn what he has to say. If he feels that way I should like to know where he was when Margaret was killed. What can you tell me of him?'

'Very little, save that he is a man of few friends.'

'Because of his manner?'

'Poor law overseers are not popular.'

'But you are one yourself now.'

'I am and I wish I were not. It is not farmers who set the payment rate for paupers and make it so small they go hungry. It is not farmers who decide that an old widow-woman must be removed to her place of settlement, a place she may not have seen since she came here as a young bride. It was not farmers who built the Woodside Poor House and said the poor must enter it or starve. But it is farmers who are made overseers of the poor and have to carry these things out on behalf of their betters, and farmers who get the blame. When a labourer has no work and must go to the mines or see his children sent as apprentices to some place from which they will likely never return, it is a farmer who has to tell him. Our people go off to the towns and the pit villages and they do not like it and they blame us.'

'I am sorry.'

'And when enclosure comes...'

'...and it *will* come, as it has come everywhere...'

'...people will see some farmers with big farms and many small men driven from the land. It will be the Bishop of Durham's doing, and the Blacketts' doing, and it is they who make money from enclosures but it is us the people see and us they blame. People have long memories. They remember not only their own grievances but those of their fathers and their grandfathers.'

'I notice you are careful to blame the Bishop and the Blacketts but not your own landlord, Lord Ravenshead. Or me.'

Tom said nothing.

'And that is the only reason Maughan is not liked?'

'No, sir. I am sorry, I mean, No. In his case, people are right to blame the farmer. Walter Maughan is not a mean man but he is a terror with paupers. You know here before the Poor House the pauper's allowance was three pound and eighteen shilling for a year. One shilling and sixpence – eighteen pence, Mister Blakiston – to feed and clothe themselves for a week.'

'It is not much, Tom.'

'It is less than not much; it is close to nothing at all. But Walter Maughan said the better off sort in the parish should not be asked to pay so much and he wanted to reduce the allowance to one shilling. Two pound twelve shilling in a whole year. Twelve pence for a week at a time when meat is ninepence a pound and you would pay three pence for a loaf of bread.'

'But, Tom, the Law sets the allowances and they are more than that.'

'That is no help to those who cannot pay a lawyer.'

'Well, it is disgraceful.'

'The Rector prevented him from carrying it through. But still, it is not possible to be a poor law overseer and be liked by people and I wish I had not been elected. I will be glad when my term of office is over. Which is not something ever said by Walter Maughan, for he loves the work so much he takes the turn of others. Do you know, when Henry Foster died we removed his widow Mary and their two children. Just for the removal expenses and the cost of the hearing at the Sessions we paid eight pound, three shilling and five pence. For that we could have kept all three on the parish till the year after next, and kept the bairns where they know and are known instead of some place they never saw. And we could have gone on keeping them another three year after that, had we but asked Mary's settlement parish to bear the cost of keeping them here instead of having to receive a woman they had no desire ever to see again and her two young ones. At the end of that time the children would have grown to working age and the woman likely remarried.'

'Did you suggest it?'

'I did. Walter Maughan said that is not how things are done. What he meant is that he would not pass up a chance to make more miserable lives that were already almost too hard to bear.'

It was with those words fresh in his mind that Blakiston rode to the fertile land beyond Bradley Fell where Walter Maughan farmed almost five hundred acres – a big farm by Durham standards. Maughan's landlord was the Bishop of Durham and not Lord Ravenshead, so Blakiston had no authority there and was unsure how he would be received. He had seen the man at church but exchanged no words with him.

He need not have worried. Maughan was in the fields supervising the wheat harvest but when a boy brought word of a visitor he left his sons in charge and rode to the house. He came into the kitchen, a tall powerful man in a hurry, threw his three-cornered hat on the table, seized Blakiston by the elbow and hauled him to his feet. 'Good God, man, have they left you in here? Come through to the parlour like the gentleman you are.' He turned to the maid who hovered in the doorway. 'Coffee for Mister Blakiston. And is there any of that fruit cake left?' Then he looked at Blakiston. 'Or would you rather take a glass of small beer, sir?'

The force of the entry and welcome had knocked Blakiston out of his normal calm. 'Mister Maughan. You are kind, but this is not a social call.'

Maughan raised an eyebrow but said nothing.

'You have not heard the news? About your daughter, Margaret?'

'That wanton is no daughter of mine. What has she done now?'

'She is dead, sir. Murdered.'

The silence lasted a minute at least, and what went on behind Maughan's suddenly immobile face Blakiston could not have said. Then the farmer turned again to the serving maid, whose hand was over her mouth. Quietly he said, 'Call your mistress, Nell. We will be in the parlour. Then coffee, cake and cheese. Quickly now.'

He took Blakiston's elbow once more, gently this time, and guided him into a room that was one third the size of the big kitchen but made lighter by white wallpaper dotted with small red and blue flowers. On three sides of the room were solid wooden settles covered by green cloth cushions, with a low table occupying the space between them. The fourth wall was dominated by a fireplace though no fire burned in it at this warmest time of the year.

The door opened and a tall, subdued woman entered. Maughan took her immediately by the hand. 'Mister Blakiston, this is Jane, my wife. Jane, Mister Blakiston.' Jane Maughan nodded in Blakiston's direction. Maughan had not let go of her hand. 'You have heard? About Margaret?'

'Nell told me.' The voice was gentle, well modulated – and not from these parts, thought Blakiston. She turned towards him. 'Please, Mister Blakiston, sit. And then I should like to hear what happened to Margaret.'

At that point, Nell and another girl came in carrying trays which they arranged on the table. 'Thank you,' said Jane. 'You may leave service to me.' The two maids curtseyed and left the room. Jane poured coffee into three cups and handed one each to Blakiston and her husband. She cut two slices from the fruitcake and topped each with a slice of cheese. These were for the men only; she ate nothing herself. She looked expectantly at Blakiston. 'Who killed her? Was it her husband?'

'I have arrested him for it, though he denies being the killer. But really I am intrigued, for this happened on Saturday morning or even on Friday night and I know you were in church on Sunday and the whole parish must have known by then. I should have told you myself had I had any reason to connect Margaret Laws with you. Did you hear nothing till now?'

Husband and wife shook their heads. Maughan said, 'We have our own pew in church.'

'I know, for I have seen you in it.'

'The rector does not like it that a farmer has a pew of his own but it was bought and paid for by my father before Reverend Claverley came here. Probably someone else's servants would have told ours, and we should have learned from them, but our maids and hired men share the pew with us.' He sniffed. 'The rector likes that even less, but it is a master's duty to see that his people worship God in His house and that they are not distracted by idle chitter-chatter while they do it. I am sorry, Mister Blakiston, but I must ask you to take it on yourself to tell us what you know.'

Blakiston nodded. 'I shall do so, though I fear it is little enough.' When he had finished, Maughan said, 'You do not seem sure that Joseph Laws is guilty of her murder.'

'If he is not, I do not understand why he attacked me. Or why he ran away. But I am vexed by this question of the letter. At first it seemed easy: he told me that there had been a letter, telling him to go to Carlisle, and I believed that either the letter had not existed or that he had written it himself to give substance to his story. But he cannot write…'

'But Margaret could, and she might have written the letter herself to get him away from the house, while the maid would also be gone…'

'…and that is also true and crossed my mind. But I had the constable ask the postboy and there was a letter and the postboy did deliver it.'

'It could still have been sent by Margaret. She got him out of the house so that she could pursue her strumpet's impulses, and Joseph returned before the man had left and so he killed her.'

'Then why go to the trouble of posting it, when she could simply have shown it to him? And why does he say nothing of finding a man in his place? No, Maughan, it does not hold. But I fear Joseph Laws must stay where he is till we find ourselves on clearer ground. It is an uncomfortable lodging he has found.'

'That is no more than he should expect. God's will is not set aside without retribution.'

'I'm sorry?'

'The Book of Proverbs, Mister Blakiston. Whoso loveth wisdom rejoiceth his father: but he that keepeth company with harlots spendeth his substance. Joseph Laws married my daughter, a proven Jezebel, to get the tenancy of a farm. He wasted his Heavenly treasure for the transitory gains of this sinful world.'

Blakiston glanced at the farmer's wife. She had not spoken since giving him the coffee and cake; if she had any reservations about the picture her husband painted of their daughter, it did not show on her face. 'Well, Maughan,' he said. 'I must be about my business.'

Now Jane Maughan spoke at last. 'When is the funeral to be?'

'That I do not know,' said Blakiston. 'Nor who will arrange it.'

'We will do that,' she said, and now it was Maughan who received Blakiston's quick glance but he showed no sign of disagreeing with his wife. 'It is not fair to expect Tom Laws to pay,' he said. 'And I would not saddle the parish with the cost.'

The words interrupted Blakiston's intention to leave. 'Mister Maughan,' he said. 'I shall speak plainly and I ask that you treat my questions in a spirit of openness. You have welcomed me in a most generous and warm-hearted way, and yet you have the reputation …' He tailed off as Maughan's eyebrows rose, but the expression he saw was one of amusement and not annoyance.

'The reputation,' he went on, 'of a man who is the scourge of paupers. And here you are saying that you will bear a cost to save the parish.'

Amusement had now become an open smile on Maughan's face. 'I know what people say about me, Mister Blakiston. Sit down. Let us drink another cup of coffee and talk about what you have said.'

In truth, Blakiston was pressed for time and did not feel that he had enough to spend in this way, but he wanted to hear what the man had to say. He did, though, refuse the offer of more coffee.

Maughan said, 'You know that Our Lord said, "The poor you have always with you".'

'I do. To be frank, I have often wondered why a God who has all power in His hands should not trouble to change that.'

'It would not serve His holy purpose. The poor are not poor by chance. Look in our own parish; the evidence is there. Tom Laws, Joseph's brother, was born the second son of a farmer. The way things are now, with enclosure coming and fewer men needed on a farm, his fate was clear; to pick up work as he could and live each day from hand to mouth, or to leave the land for the brutish life of the coal mines. But the Laws have always been a good and God-fearing family and see how he has been rewarded; when Wrekin, son of your master under God Lord Ravenshead, ravished Lizzie Greener and left her with child, God chose Tom Laws to take the dishonoured maid as his wife and the babe as his own, and rewarded him with the tenancy of Chopwell Garth.'

Blakiston coughed. 'In fact, it was I who chose Tom Laws to get the farm.'

'It was God acting through you, Mister Blakiston. And the Greeners, too, desperate poor though they were, have always been a Christian family and they have had their reward.'

'The rape of a daughter? That is God's reward for their piety?'

'Lizzie is become a farmer's wife. She could never have hoped for that. And her mother, Florrie, lives her final years in comfort with maids to order about when she must have expected to age and die a penniless crone.'

'In fact,' said his wife, 'Florrie is Lizzie's stepmother. But I agree, she is a good person. And her daughter Kate, Lizzie's sister, is the most perfect young woman you could meet on a long day's walk and she, too, is blessed for she must now find a husband to thank God for.'

'And all this,' said Maughan, 'from what you call the rape of a daughter. Inexcusable though that was.'

'And how will God deal with the rapist for it?'

Maughan passed a hand across his face. 'It is not for the likes of me to forecast God's way with the son of a baron. Wrekin will know his fate in due time.'

Blakiston had been a non-believer for the last ten of his twenty-six years but there were few people with whom he felt able to let down his guard and he did not judge Maughan to be one of them. 'I was brought up,' he said, 'to believe that God helps those who help themselves.'

Maughan spread his hands and smiled. 'Then look at Job King. He was born here into absolute poverty. But see him now. Others were content to eke out a few joyless years at the parish's expense. Indeed, his own brothers and sisters did so and they died in poverty. But Job took himself off to America. I know nothing of what he did there but he has prospered for here he is, not fifty years old and back among us the tenant of Gaskell Lodge.'

'A handsome estate,' said Blakiston. 'If small.'

'And set to become more so, Mister Blakiston, for Job is returned with all sorts of New World ways and notions and the money to put them into practice. Already we feel the effect, for he is hiring people for the harvest and paying them by the acre and not by the day. And unheard of sums. I am told he agreed with old Dick Jackson that Dick would reap fifteen acres of wheat and be paid five shillings the acre. *And* he will have his beer and allowances. He is paying the other men the same.'

'That will be expensive wheat.'

'We shall see, Mister Blakiston. I shall be watching this experiment with great interest.'

'You have told me how God rewards the virtuous, Maughan. But what of the undeserving?'

'We must not let people starve and the Act for the Relief of the Poor does not allow us to. People who cannot work must be provided for. People who can work must be made to do so. But people who will not work should be cared for only in prison. That is what the law says, Mister Blakiston, and it is good law.'

Into Blakiston's mind came words he had heard in church so many times: "Blessed be the poor, for theirs is the kingdom of God." But he felt weary at the thought of debating further with a man more convinced of the rightness of his ideas than Blakiston could imagine ever being. He stood. 'It has been a fascinating conversation, Maughan. But I must take my leave.'

Chapter 11

Heavily though it lay on Blakiston's mind, Margaret's murder would get little attention that week. The business of the wheat harvest left him no time for investigation.

He rode to Chopwell Garth for the discussion with Tom Laws and Jeffrey Drabble on how the work was to be carried out. Drabble was already there, having walked from New Hope Farm, and Blakiston was impressed as he had been many times before by the dogged refusal of Ryton's poor to allow their circumstances to overwhelm them. He asked Lizzie to send her brother Ned to join them for he, too, had a part to play.

Florrie told Nellie, the maid, to bring small beer for the visitors. Then she left them alone.

'I have decided,' Blakiston said, 'that the best way to deal with this is to treat the two farms as one.'

'Do you mean always?' asked Tom.

'At this moment I mean for the purposes of the wheat harvest. Later we will see. Chopwell Garth and New Hope would make a single farm of nearly six hundred acres and that may be too much for you to handle, Tom. But for the harvest it will work well. We have one hundred and twenty acres of wheat on the two farms together. If we say that one man can reap fifteen acres, we need eight men. Drabble makes one and Ned another and we agreed at the Whitsuntide fair with five more. They are working now at the home farm and they should be here on Thursday, which is three days from now. We need one more. Joseph's hired man was to be that one, but Joseph chose to get rid of him.'

'Perhaps he will come back,' said Tom. 'Now that Joseph is gone.'

'Perhaps he will. I need to talk to him anyway, to see what he has to say about Margaret Laws and his relations with her.'

'Beg pardon, Master,' said Drabble, 'but I am constable this year. What will I do if something happens that needs the constable?'

'We shall deal with that question when it arises, Drabble. Until it does, you will work all the hours of daylight on the harvest. Unless it rains, of course. Our agreement with the men was that they would have their pay at the end of each day and that applies also to you. You will eat and sleep at New Hope Farm, as we have agreed with that bad-tempered young woman there, but the hired men will sleep in the barns, six to each farm, and they are entitled each day to bread, cheese and five pints of ale and half a pound of beef for each one. Tom, the cook at the home farm will bake the beef into pies, which the men prefer. Could you please speak to Lizzie and Florrie about doing the same here? And I will instruct Susannah Ward.'

Tom nodded. 'They will be expecting no less.'

'The men are also to be supplied with gloves. The Castle has seen to the making of those and I shall bring them when next I come. The harvest will be by reaping, not mowing, and as close to the ground as possible. Drabble, when I came to New Hope yesterday I saw you with a scythe in your hand.'

'I was practising, Master. Reaping is not as easy as it was when I was young.'

'Very well. You are to be commended. Tom, your task will be to watch the men at work and make sure that they reap low, and only when the corn is dry, and that the shocks they make are sized in accordance with the number of weeds.'

'Shocks?'

'The bundles, man, that they bind the crop into.'

'We call them stooks here, Master.'

'Very well; stooks. I want them stacked so that they shake off rain, and not so close that the sun and wind cannot get in to dry them. Now. The business of transferring the crops to the farmyard. I know you have waggons on both farms. Tell me how you work them.'

'We use three. While one is loading in the field, one is unloading in the yard and the other moves back and forth between the two.'

'Three waggons means six horses.'

'We have only two here. The others come from the Castle at harvest time.'

'This year you will have only one of the Castle's horses.'

'But, Mister Blakiston...we cannot run three waggons with only three horses.'

'Nor will you need to, for we have been making carts at the Castle and three carts will come here this week. Each cart is drawn by only one horse. I am determined to bring our farms into line with the practice in the South, where waggons have not been used for some years. You will find that carts work better than waggons and with half of the horses. Drabble, you have two horses at New Hope and you will receive four more from the Castle, but next year New Hope, too, will change from waggons to carts. By next year's harvest also, both farms – or one combined farm, if that is what we decide to do – will have installed iron rails in the farmyard so that we can deliver the crop from yard to barn with no loss of grain.'

The three Durham men stared at him in amazement.

'I know that farmers believe that whatever has been the standard practice of their county has been so since time immemorial and cannot be altered,' said Blakiston. 'They are wrong. Now, gleaning. At the home farm we are not permitting gleaning to begin until the shocks – I beg your pardon, the *stooks* – have been cleared from field to yard.'

Tom said, 'The Blacketts don't allow gleaners into the fields after reaping till pigs have been allowed to graze there.'

'I know the Blacketts do that, and so does the Bishop of Durham, and we will not follow their example because it is an iniquitous practice. The poor have had the right in England for as long as records have been kept to go into the fields and glean the grain that is left behind by the scythe. It is a right they have by permission of the farmer, but it is a right nevertheless and to deprive them of it by giving first pick to hogs is a dirty trick. Especially when the poor are under such oppression otherwise. But the poor have begun to glean from the stooks themselves and that is not to continue. As soon as the stooks have been cleared away, the fields will be opened to gleaners.'

There was a loud clatter from the farmyard and Blakiston said, 'That sound you hear brings me to the last thing I want to tell you today. Come into the yard with me and I shall show you what is afoot.'

They followed him outside, to find two men unloading rough wooden planks and a collection of bricks from a cart. Blakiston said, 'The same delivery is being made to New Hope Farm. The sheaves will be taken into the barn which is what, next year, you will have the iron rails in place for. Stacking them on a wooden floor, raised on bricks, will protect them from rats and keep them free of dampness from the floor and so we will lose less than in the past. You and Ned, Drabble, will spend the rest of the day building a floor here, and tomorrow you will both do the same at New Hope.' He walked into the barn, the three men following him. 'Build the floor against this wall, nearest to the yard. That will leave room beyond for threshing. If there is time after you have built floors in both barns, you will also cut an opening – a sort of window, but with shutters and no glass – in the wall by the yard so that the sheaves can be thrown directly from the cart, through the window and onto the raised floor. Tom Laws, as Drabble is to work here today I take it you can give him his dinner?

'He can eat in the kitchen with us.'

'Excellent. Are there any questions, or shall I leave you to begin?'

Before he left Chopwell Garth, Blakiston sought out Kate and walked with her from the dairy to the farmhouse door. 'Dearest Kate, please tell me you are not altered in your intentions.'

'I am not so changeable, James.' She smiled up at him, that sweet smile through her eyelashes that reduced him to a jelly. 'I said you may have our banns read on Sunday, and you may.' She rested a hand on his arm. 'Will you stay for dinner?'

'I cannot. His Lordship wishes to see me and before that I must find Emmett Batey and ask what passed between him and Joseph's wife.'

As he took the reins in his hand and climbed into the saddle he saw Jeffrey Drabble's eyes fixed on both of them. Drabble had seen the hand on his arm and the smile his beloved gave him; no doubt he had not failed also to notice the besotted look on his own face. Well, at the end of the week there need be no more dissembling. He had promised Kate to keep all secret until their banns were read for the first time in church, but then everyone would know of their love.

When he arrived at the hovel that was home to Emmett Batey's mother she told him that her son had gone to Philadelphia to look for work in the pits.

'Has he a horse?'

'No, Master, he walked.

'But that must be fifteen miles from here.'

'And fifteen miles back, Master. But what choice does he have if we are not to starve?'

'Does he want to work in a coal mine?'

'He wants to stay above ground as his father and his grandfather did. But Joseph Laws got rid of him and it will be months before the next hiring fair.'

'If he can start by the end of this week he has no need to wait for a fair, for I have a job for him. Tell him to present himself at my house at seven in the morning. If not tomorrow, because he spends the night at Philadelphia, then the day after tomorrow. If I do not hear from him by then I will find someone else and the opportunity will be lost.'

'Sir, I will send his younger brother to tell him.'

'How old is the boy?'

'He is thirteen, Master. His name is Robert.'

'Thirteen. Has he time to fetch his brother? Is he not working?'

'He works when he can, Master. He was passed over at the Whitsun hiring fair.'

'Very well, Mistress Batey. Send him. If Emmett Batey is at my house at seven, tomorrow morning or the morning after, we have work for him.'

As Blakiston rode away, he thought how much he would have liked to add the words, "and for his brother Robert" to "we have work for him". Times were hard for those without land, and getting harder. He was confident in what he was doing; future generations would be grateful for the larger farms, the transfer of strips of land in common ownership to more effective units, the modern farming methods that meant fewer people could produce bigger crops. Better agriculture would make the country richer, and so would the mining and manufacturing industries that were growing as men and women no longer needed on the land expanded the workforce in the towns and pit villages. Still, many of the people who had worked the land were paying a terrible price now for the benefits others would have in the future.

The rector would say that all was ordered for the best in God's world, and the poor would have their reward in the life to come. Walter Maughan on the other hand would say that the poor were being punished by God for sins known to Him though invisible to us. But these comforts were not available to Blakiston.

Giving work to a thirteen-year-old would be an act of charity – a good act. But where would it end? It was a fact that there was not enough work to go round, and employing someone who was not really needed would solve no problems and would damage his own master's interests. A thought that reminded him that Lord Ravenshead was waiting to see him at Ravenshead Castle. He urged Obsidian into a gallop.

He gave Obsidian into the care of one of the stable boys and stopped in the kitchen, as he always did, to check his appearance in the glass. Then he made his way along stone-floored passageways till he came to the family's quarters where he climbed carpeted stairs two at a time and entered Lord Ravenshead's Business Office.

His Lordship was deep in the examination of two maps that lay on his desk. 'Blakiston! It is good to see you.' He gestured towards a sideboard. 'Help yourself to coffee. You might pour a cup for me while you are about it.'

Blakiston did as he was told, taking at the same time two pieces of Scottish shortbread sweetened with caraways and orange peel. His breakfast seemed suddenly a long time in the past. He had drunk the coffee and eaten both pieces of shortbread before Lord Ravenshead wrote a note on the bottom of one of the maps, signed it with a flourish and looked up. 'So, Blakiston. What I really want to talk about is the wheat harvest. But first you had better tell me the news of this poor woman who was done to death on one of our farms – Margaret Laws, was it not? I understand you have her husband under arrest.'

'I have, my Lord, or rather he is under arrest for I have no authority in the matter. But he says he did not kill his wife and I am inclined to believe him.'

'That is bad news.'

'My Lord?'

'Blakiston, there could hardly be a busier time in a farm overseer's life than August and September. I was happy to see you find the killers of Reuben Cooper and I would not prevent you from seeking the solution to this new mystery, but if one is already in your hands I should prefer you to give your attention to the efficient working of my Estate.'

'My Lord…'

'Do not misunderstand me; I should not wish to see an innocent man hang so that we can be sure of getting the grain into the barns before the weather breaks. But the Durham Assize takes place in the first week of August, which means it has just passed for the year and Joseph Laws cannot now stand trial until fifty more weeks have passed – is that not correct?'

'It is, my Lord. And a miserable fifty weeks it will be.'

'Yes, I dare say, and if he is guilty that is no more than he deserves and if he is innocent then it is a shame. But this estate is responsible for many more people than one tenant farmer and it is my wish that misery should be suffered by as few of those as possible, so please leave Laws where he is until the harvest is safely in. You may spend five pounds each month, if you think it necessary, to ensure that he does not lack for necessities.'

'Thank you, my Lord.'

There was a discreet knock at the door, which opened immediately to admit Harris, Lord Ravenshead's butler. 'Beg pardon, my Lord. News has just come to the servants' quarters which, knowing Mister Blakiston was here, I felt you and he would wish to hear without delay.'

'Yes? Out with it.'

'My Lord, Ezra Hindmarsh is dead.'

'Who the devil is Ezra Hindmarsh?' asked Ravenshead.

Blakiston shook his head. 'I never heard the name.'

'His father is a tenant on a Blackett farm.'

'A Blackett farm?' repeated Ravenshead. 'Then what has this to do with Mister Blakiston?'

'My Lord, the boy was strangled.'

'Oh, no. You are going to tell me he died as Margaret Laws died? That we have one killer who does not stop at a single victim?'

'It would seem so, my Lord.'

Ravenshead turned his eyes to the ceiling. 'You will have to investigate, Blakiston. But, please, do not be distracted from the harvest.'

Chapter 12

He had expected a greater feeling of satisfaction. When you have dreamed of revenge for so long, achieving it should surely gratify more. If he were honest—if he looked into his heart and examined what was really there and not what he told himself should be there – he had felt compassion for the boy and revulsion at what he himself was doing.

He had done it nevertheless – put his strong hands around the defenceless boy's neck and broken it – and he would not allow himself to regret it. He would not. Revenge is necessary, the way the world has been for ever, a fundamental law of nature.

No-one had had mercy on George. Or Mary. Or the others. The lesson had been there for anyone who cared to learn it.

His Lordship wanted the harvest to have the overseer's attention before all else and he was right to want that. Blakiston rode to the home farm. William Welton, who had the tenancy there, was a man not always in tune with Blakiston's views on modern farming but he had the wheat harvest well under control.

'You will be finished with the day labourers on time?' asked Blakiston.

'Aye, Master. All will be done by Wednesday night, so only it does not rain before then.'

'The crop is still ahead of last year's?'

We have nearly one third as much again. And the grains are fatter in the ear. That will be the rain we had all those nights in July, with the sun in the day.'

'A good harvest, then. Is there ought you wish to tell me?'

Hesitation was visible on Welton's face. 'Master. This matter of the wheat among the turnips.'

'Yes? Out with it, man. You doubt the practice?'

'You want us to sow wheat between the rows of turnips, after we have weeded them. I never heard of such a thing, Master. And nor has anyone else.'

'This would be a poor land, Welton, with no possibility of improvement, if we never did a new thing because no Ryton farmer has heard of it.'

'But...'

'A Mister Walker does it and gets good crops without paying for tillage. We shall try it here, because this land has a sandy nature and so does the Norfolk farm of Mister Walker.'

'But, sir, when we set the sheep in to eat the turnips, will they not have the wheat as well?'

'Walker says his do not.'

'But...'

'Enough, Welton. If all falls to disaster you may laugh with your friends about the overseer's foolishness. But try it we will. Is that all?'

Welton raised both hands in a gesture of defeat. 'There is nought else, Master.'

'Then tell me where is the farm that Ezra Hindmarsh's father works.'

Ezra Hindmarsh's father is dead, Master. His wife also. The fever took them both. The boy lived with his grandfather.'

'And his name?'

'Ezra, Master. The boy was named for his father's father.'

When Blakiston arrived there, he found Ezra Hindmarsh the grandfather in the lowest of spirits. 'I am sorry for your loss,' he said.

'Aye. Thank you, Overseer. It seems this is a time for loss, for it is not twelve month since the boy's parents went, and his two sisters, and now him. But God took those others and some man killed Ezra.'

'Did the boy have enemies?'

'He was nine years old.'

'You are right. It was a foolish question and I apologise for asking it.'

'Do I have enemies, you should rightly have asked. And I can only say that if I have enemies who would do this then I do not know who they may be. But I am a Blackett tenant and you are Lord Ravenshead's man. Why are you here asking these things?'

'You had heard of the death of Margaret Laws?'

'Her that was Walter Maughan's girl? Aye. But what has she to do with this?'

'She was killed in the same way.'

'You think who killed her killed Ezra? But surely...I had thought...everyone thought...her death was the chastisement of a harlot. And did I not hear that you had Joseph Laws locked up for it? If he is in Durham jail he could not have killed our Ezra.'

'He is in Durham jail but he says he did not murder his wife and I am inclined to believe him.'

A woman so toothless that Blakiston guessed she must be at least sixty but standing upright like one much younger came into the room. 'Mister Blakiston, welcome. Forgive my husband's manners for he grieves for young Ezra. Can I offer you small beer? Bread? Cheese?'

'Thank you, Mistress Hindmarsh, nothing for me. I wonder, could I see where the boy died?'

'It was not here,' said Hindmarsh. 'He went every morning to the Misses Carrick and he was killed as he rode home.'

'You had him in school! That is commendable.'

'Aye, we thought to give him a more educated life. Now he has no life at all.'

'And he went and came back on horseback?'

'A pony, for he was no age. But a good animal and one he cared for. It was when the pony came home alone that I went to look for the boy and found him in the churchyard. I carried him to Doctor Barraclough but there was nought to be done.'

'The churchyard. I wonder, would you show me the exact place?'

The old man's face said he would rather not go back there but he stood, nevertheless. 'My horse will not carry me as fast as that magnificent black of yours. You will need to go at my pace.'

As they rode side by side, Blakiston said, 'Was the boy doing well at school?'

'The Carrick ladies were pleased with him. He was a good boy. What you asked him to do, he did. And we wanted him to hold his head a little higher, you know, than we have been able to do.'

'School would give him that?'

'He could already read and write and do his sums. Farmers must take their turn as overseers of the poor and my time was more difficult than it might have been because I could not write, and nor could I understand what was put in front of me without someone told me what it said.'

'I am hearing a lot about the job of the overseer.'

'I hated it, Master. It must be done, I know that, but it is hard to have to decide the fate of those less fortunate than you.'

'Walter Maughan says that overseers do God's work.'

'Walter Maughan may say what he likes. In my view, we did the work of our betters who did not want to spend more than they must.'

Blakiston refrained from asking whether Hindmarsh's "betters" included his landlords the Blacketts; the man had suffered enough with the death of his grandson. 'You will have meant the tenancy of the farm to go to the boy?'

'We hoped to live long enough for that to happen. Now…'

'I think you have considered this.'

'I have. If I fall ill…or my wife does…or if the Blacketts decide I am too old…then the overseers of the poor will be upon us in our turn.'

'Well, I shall hope that things go well with you.' As he spoke, Blakiston felt the emptiness of the words and was glad that they had reached the churchyard and he could turn the conversation to other matters.

Hindmarsh dismounted and went without speaking to a patch of land without gravestones; only bumps in the grass told what lay beneath. Blakiston followed him. 'He was here,' said the old man.

'On this grave? Exactly on it?'

'Yes, Master. He lay on the mound, his head at this end and his feet there.'

'I wonder whether that was by chance? And, if not, whose grave this is?'

'I'm sorry, Master, I cannot say. But here is the rector. He may know.'

Blakiston turned towards the path that led into the churchyard from the rectory and saw a frown on Thomas's usually carefree face. 'Ezra Hindmarsh,' said Thomas. 'Lady Isabella said she saw you here and I have hurried to condole with you.'

The old man looked blankly at the rector, and even Blakiston paused to wonder whether he had ever heard that word "condole" before. Thomas went on, 'We brought nothing into this world, and it is certain we can carry nothing out. The Lord gave, and the Lord hath taken away; blessed be the name of the Lord. But it is hard to lose one so young. Have you decided when the funeral should be?'

'I...I...we have not thought, Rector.'

'Really, it should be done by Thursday. Shall we say at ten? Where is the body now?'

Hindmarsh's face was so contorted, Blakiston would not have been surprised to see him cry. As much to protect the man from what seemed heartless as because he wanted the information, he said, 'Thomas, before we settle that, can you tell us who lies in this grave? Because this is where Ezra Hindmarsh found his grandson.'

The rector looked where Blakiston pointed. 'I really could not say. This area, you know, is for paupers' graves. Whoever was buried here was paid for by the parish and the parish does not meet the cost of a stone.'

'There is no record? Of who was buried where?'

'In a perfect world, of course...but we live in a world that is far from perfection. There will be a name in the register for everyone buried here since the fifteen hundreds but that will not tell us where a body was interred and without knowing the date we cannot tell which body lies in which grave.'

'The sexton would know?'

'He would, but unless these bodies were buried less than eight years ago, which from the condition of the graves I doubt, he will have taken the knowledge to his own grave. Martin Bolam was the sexton before the one we have now,' he said, noting Blakiston's puzzled look, 'and he is dead. Now, Ezra. Where is the body?'

'With the carpenter, Rector.'

'Which carpenter? Matthew Rainbow? Ezekiah Dunn?'

'Matthew, Rector.'

'Good. Shall I instruct him to have the coffin here on Wednesday afternoon, that is tomorrow, so that it can sit all night in the church? I expect you would like to come and keep vigil? And then we can bury him the next morning. Does that sound right?'

Hindmarsh nodded. To Blakiston, he said, 'Sir, if you have no further need of me I should get home. Florrie will be grieving alone.'

Blakiston bent and picked up a red rose. 'Was this here when you found your grandson's body?'

'Yes, Master. I thought nothing of it—mebbes the lad was carrying it. You think he could have been killed for stealing a rose?'

'No, Ezra,' said Thomas. 'Someone laid a rose just like this here a few days ago. It has nothing to do with young Ezra. Get off, now, and give your wife what comfort you can.'

When the old man had gone, Thomas said, 'James, you think me lacking in compassion. Don't deny it, man; it is written in your face.'

'I think…'

'Let us discuss it on Sunday at dinner. We may see what our other guests have to say. Lord Ravenshead, my master under God and yours *in toto*, has sent for me and I must be gone. I paused only to see poor old Ezra. For whom I do grieve, James, whatever you may think.'

Blakiston nodded his agreement. 'And I must see what the doctor has to tell me about the state of the boy's body when it was brought to him.'

The rector took his watch from his pocket and looked at it. 'Well, it is still but early. Barraclough may yet be sober enough to speak sense to you.'

And sober the doctor was – but of little use for all that. Speaking clearly in unslurred words he told Blakiston that the boy had been strangled, for small bones in his neck were broken and his head hung to one side; that he had no way of knowing whether the murderer had been man or woman, tall or short, young or adult; and that, no, there was no sign of old bruising on the body.

As Blakiston mounted Obsidian and rode away he found himself wishing that the dead boy's pony could speak – for it alone seemed to have witnessed its master's death. He also wondered why Lord Ravenshead had called for the rector's presence.

Chapter 13

Next morning was Thursday, the thirtieth of August. When Blakiston answered the door to the usual knock to say his breakfast was here, a man he had never seen before was waiting behind the inn's serving maid. 'Are you here to see me?'

'Yes, sir. Emmett Batey, Sir.'

'Ah, yes. Batey.' The man's clothes were scarcely more than rags but they were clean and his face was clean-shaven but nothing could hide the hunger in his gaunt features. Blakiston spoke to the maid who had placed his tray on the kitchen table and was about to leave. 'We will be two for breakfast, Betty. Bring another tray. As quickly as you can, now. Come in, Batey. Sit down, man.'

Emmett Batey sat at the table on the chair Blakiston had indicated, his round hat on his knee. He looked ill at ease.

'So. If you are here this early, I take it you want to work on the harvest?'

'Yes, sir. If it please you, Sir.'

'It will please me greatly since we are a man short and you know one of the farms on which you will be working. And here is Betty. Well done, girl. Set it down in front of Mister Batey.' He took a sixpenny piece from his purse and pressed it into her hand. 'Now, Mister Batey, it will give me pleasure if you will join me at breakfast while we talk.'

Batey looked astonished at the generous portions of bread, butter, ham and cheese laid out before him.

'Eat, man, for I cannot sit here and breakfast alone while you watch. You will take tea with me?'

The man drained the cup and then fell on the food with such glee that Blakiston found himself taking extra pleasure in his own repast. 'You are a trencherman!'

'Sir?'

'I mean that you enjoy your food.'

'Sir, I cannot remember when I last ate this well.'

'Well, enjoy it, and while we eat I shall thank you to tell me what you can of Margaret Laws.' The shock on Batey's face was clear to see but Blakiston ignored it. 'She was the mistress when you worked at New Hope Farm. Come, man, don't let our conversation keep you from your meal. But she was the mistress, was she not?'

'Yes, Sir.' He spoke through a mouthful of ham.

'Was there any commerce between you? I mean, beyond the ordinary dealings of farmer's wife and hired man? Batey, I do not wish to have to repeat everything I say. I am not here to sit in judgement but merely to find out what happened. I have heard suggestions that you may have known

Mistress Laws in a manner normally confined to the marriage bed. Is there any truth in that?'

Batey had stopped eating entirely. His head hung down. Quietly, he said, 'Sir, she would not rest until I had her.'

'Well, if that is how it was then that is how it was. Did her husband know?'

The voice was even quieter now. 'Sir, that is why he told me to go.'

'Thank you, Batey. That is what I wanted to know. You are not in trouble, though I may wish to speak to you again when I have confronted Joseph Laws. And now finish your breakfast with a glad heart for you have done what a man should do and told the truth though it hurt you to do so.'

The next three days continued as dry and sunny as the previous weeks and the harvest occupied everyone. For Kate it involved long hours helping Florrie and Lizzie prepare food for the workers – their "allowances" – taking it out to the fields at dinner time and cleaning and making beds where the men were sleeping. She saw Blakiston only from a distance but doubted whether he had any time to spare on investigating two murders.

And then it was Sunday.

Kate was in church before anyone else and took a seat at the back. When the rector came in he laid a hand gently on her shoulder and smiled. It was probably the first time she had known him look at her as anything other than an object and she was suffused by a feeling of warmth and happiness. 'Is it going to be all right?' she whispered.

'God is with you, Kate Greener.' He passed on towards the vestry.

As the church filled up, Kate watched the congregation. The better off occupied the private pews as they always did and Kate smiled when she saw young Susannah Bent looking around at the lower classes in that sniffy, superior way she had. What a shock that young madam was about to get. Then Blakiston entered, touched Kate's arm for a second and walked on towards the pew set aside for the estate's officials but which for now only he occupied. Kate put a hand over her mouth as she remembered what would be expected of her next week. A Greener in a private pew! The rector must hope God would not strike the church with a thunderbolt. As Blakiston took his place, Kate watched Susannah Bent go through the same motions as she did every Sunday: eyes lowered, a becoming blush on her cheek, bonnet high on her forehead, her head moved round so that any man less unaware than Kate's James would have known that he was being courted. But Blakiston, for all that Kate had so recently pointed out to him Susannah's interest, seemed oblivious.

The service wound its usual slow way. The rector's sermon seemed to last for ever. Was it chance that led him to speak on the subject of the rich being cast down and the poor receiving their just reward? At last it was over and was that...was it possible...yes, the rector had given James an almost undetectable signal and James rose from his pew, walked back to where she was sitting and took his place beside her and now the rector was smiling broadly as he began to speak the words she had so longed to hear but had feared she never would. "I publish the banns of marriage between James Blakiston, late of Burley parish in the county of Hampshire and now of this parish and Catherine Greener of this parish. This is the first time of asking. If any of you know cause or just impediment why these two persons should not be joined together in holy matrimony, ye are to declare it."

Pandemonium. Hubbub so loud it drowned the rector's final sentence. Was that a screech from Susannah Bent? Actually out loud, for all to hear? It was. But almost the whole congregation was talking, heads now bent towards each other and now turned to stare at her and James sitting side by side, James looking pleased with life and she, she knew, radiating uncertainty at what they had stirred up. The rector coughed and, when there was no fall in the volume of chatter, he raised his voice. 'All stand.' And all did, and with bowed head they received his blessing, but still the buzz continued.

When they were outside, the first person to speak to the betrothed couple was Lady Isabella, who hugged Kate to her. Standing in line behind Isabella was Jane Maughan, her husband in close attendance. 'Mister Blakiston,' said Walter Maughan, 'you are a rogue.' But he said it with a smile. 'When you called to tell us of Margaret's death, we gave you our opinion of the Greener family, and of this young lady in particular, and you said not a word.' He reached out and seized Blakiston's hand, shaking it vigorously. 'Well, my dear sir, I congratulate you.' He looked behind him to where the Bents were leaving the church. 'But I fear goodwill may not be universal.' Kate, wondering what the Maughans had had to say about her, allowed herself a quick glance at Susannah Bent's face. The expression there was murderous. As she hurried past them she gave Blakiston a look of scorn but her eyes when she turned them on Kate were full of hatred. Her distressed mother was struggling to keep up, but she paused as she came to the knot of people around Kate and James. Kate felt sure she was about to receive a withering blast but Mistress Bent laid a hand on her arm and her smile was warm, if a little sad. 'My dear, my daughter has lost something she had no reason to believe would ever be hers. One day I hope she will congratulate you as I do now.' With that, she leaned close to Kate and placed a kiss on her cheek. 'I hope you will both be very happy.'

Then came Susannah Ward, the maid at New Hope Farm. 'Now I understand,' she said. 'I am sorry I said what I did.' Kate threw her arms round her and hugged her close.

Hanging back, Lizzie was the last to approach the pair. She looked up into James's eyes. 'Mister Blakiston, I am sorry I ever doubted you.'

Blakiston smiled. 'You had your sister's best interests at heart. But could you not, now, call me James?'

Dinner that Sunday at Chopwell Garth was an hour later than the usual time of twelve thirty because the labourers there for the harvest had to be attended to first. Florrie, Lizzie, Kate, Tom and Ned came to the table along with little Louise, known to all as Lulu and the outcome of Lizzie's violation. Without her, Tom would still be a labourer and not a farmer and they would all be living in poverty. Blakiston was not of the company; he would take dinner that evening at the rectory.

'Mister Blakiston wants me to call him James,' said Lizzie. 'I do not believe I can do that. Nor do I think he is right to ask it. Heaven help us, will you look at this girl's face? I swear she is not here with us at all.'

Kate knew that she was the "this girl" referred to and it was true that she did not really feel present as she usually did. Like someone who has been through a great loss or great triumph, she was overwhelmed by thoughts and memories and had to speak them. 'I thought I should be damned,' she said. 'I thought people would hate me. But they were so kind.'

'I don't think Susannah Bent cares much for you,' said Ned.

'No, but...her mother...and I wonder what it was that Walter Maughan and his wife had said to James about me?'

Lizzie shook her head. 'You are blessed, little sister.'

'And she deserves it,' said Florrie.

'Oh, she deserves it all right.' Lizzie rose from the bench she sat on and hugged Kate to her. 'Some of those people in church are gentry, but none of them are what is called Society. The kind of families Mister Blakiston comes from would not welcome you as you were welcomed today, and you should not mind. The chances are you will never meet them anyway.'

Lizzie was not quite right in what she said, for Lord Ravenshead at any rate was well disposed to the match. When Blakiston arrived at the rectory that evening, early as Thomas had instructed him, he asked why the rector had been called to the castle.

Thomas poured two glasses of madeira, one of which he handed to Blakiston. 'Why, to talk about you, my dear fellow.'

'Me?'

'You and the girl you intend to wed. His Lordship approves of your choice of bride.'

'I should have thought him above such matters.'

'Well, I shall tell you what he said, which was that your coming to Ryton was the best thing that has happened here for several years; that your marrying a girl of the parish will make your continued presence here more certain; and that your common sense in choosing for love and not for material gain, as the Blacketts offered you, says all that need be known about the man you are. I agreed with every word and did not tell him what a nincompoop I had made of myself. But that commotion must be our other guests arriving. Drink that down like a good fellow and let us welcome them.'

Job King and Mistress Susanna Spence had each come alone, for Susanna was widowed and as far as anyone knew King had never married. It crossed Blakiston's mind to wonder whether Lady Isabella had brought them together at her table with match-making in mind but he kept the thought to himself and it was as well that he did for they had not finished the soup before Mistress Spence was quarrelling with King. Blakiston caught the look of surreptitious amusement that Thomas cast in his direction.

'It is thirty years since you left this parish and these shores for the Americas?' Susanna asked.

Job nodded. 'I was twelve years old. I saw nothing for me here but poverty and death.'

'And now you wish to inflict the same poverty on our landowners?'

Blakiston expected a strong response from King but the man simply smiled. 'The labourer is worthy of his hire, Mistress Spence.'

'And where will he get his hire when all who might give him work are bankrupt? Mister

Blakiston, how does Lord Ravenshead regard Mister King's activities?'

Blakiston paused, shaken by the sudden challenge to join a debate he did not feel part of. 'We have not discussed it.'

'Not discussed it? A man brings foreign practices to our English farms, hostile foreign practices, and one of the biggest landowners in the county has not discussed it with his overseer?'

King was smiling. 'From what I hear, Mister Blakiston is not above bringing in foreign practices himself. I believe you have the farmers hereabouts in a tizz over your ways with wheat among the turnips.'

Blakiston had been aware of Lady Isabella's growing unease and now she intervened. 'I am sure there is a place where farming methods should be discussed,' she said. 'The rectory dinner table is probably not it. Mister King, I believe we should all learn much if you would be good enough to tell us about conditions in America.'

'Before he does that,' said Mistress Spence, 'we should perhaps join in congratulating Mister Blakiston on his engagement. It shows a courage bordering on effrontery.'

As the others murmured their agreement, Blakiston wondered whether he had just been praised or insulted. 'Thank you,' he said, nodding towards Job King. 'But I, too, would like to hear Mister King's stories of the new lands.'

King looked down as though considering what to say or where to begin. Then, as he began to speak, his eyes went round the company person by person. 'You know,' he said, 'that when I left here I was less than nothing. A pauper from a family of paupers; a difficulty to my betters. There was work in the summer but in winter the parish had to give us enough to keep us from starving.' He looked at Mistress Spence. 'Just as they do for the poor today. And some of us did starve, despite what our...betters...did to save us. I watched them, and I knew that, perhaps before long, I should be one of them. And so I took ship for Virginia. A passage would have cost six pound, but I did not have six shilling never mind six pound and so I agreed to be indentured and to work for my keep alone till the fare was paid. It was five year before I had paid the debt and became a free man. They do the same for transported felons, you know, but in their case they must work for seven year and not five.'

'Five years of servitude,' said the rector, 'and far from the people and place you knew. You must have wondered sometimes whether you would have been better off staying here.'

'Never,' said King, 'for in America I had no "betters." You are taken there for what you are and not for what your birth was. And the terms of the indentured labourer are that at the end of the five year the government gives you fifty acres of land and your employer must give you the tools to farm them.'

'That is what happened to you?' asked Blakiston.

'It is. You know, last year King George issued his Great Proclamation that forbids settlement west of the Appalachians, but when it was my turn there was no such law and my fifty acres were in Indian lands.'

Lady Isabella shuddered. 'Did you not fear for your life?'

'Perhaps I should have done for it is certain that some died. We banded together, all the settlers in the area, to help each other with the building of homes and the breaking of new land and to defend ourselves when we had to. Most of the time it was a hard life more than a dangerous one and those of us who were used to hard lives at home did well. And those who weren't went off to become clerks or storekeepers in the towns.'

'What happened to their land?' asked Blakiston.

'Sometimes they sold it to one of us. Sometimes they simply left without saying they were going; those farms we divided among ourselves.'

The rector said, 'Blakiston here will not allow a farmer to keep his tenancy unless he has a wife. You must have found the life even harder without a helpmeet?'

King nodded once and looked down and Blakiston, watching carefully, would have sworn that there was something the man was not telling them. 'In any case,' he said, 'you built a life for yourself.'

King spoke more quietly now, reinforcing Blakiston's sense that something was not being said. 'I worked every day from sun-up to sun-down. As the towns grew the price of grain and sheep and vegetables and cheese and beef rose. I spent nothing I did not have to spend except on things the farm needed. After five years I had two hundred acres. After ten, eight hundred. After fifteen, two thousand.'

'A huge spread,' said Blakiston.

'The land was there, it was fertile and it was cheap for there was more than enough to go round. If you showed you could fence it and break the sod, it was as good as given to you. It was only when you had worked it successfully that the value rose.'

As quietly as King, for he felt sympathy with the man, Blakiston said, 'You could not work two thousand acres alone.'

King was again looking down. 'I had ten men directly in my employ.' He looked up, his direct gaze addressing Mistress Spence. 'They worked hard and I made sure all were fed and paid enough that they could clothe themselves and put a little aside in case they wanted one day to do what I had done and strike out on their own. But most of the land I leased out, for that is the way in the Americas. Mostly, the people who go there are the sort who want to be their own masters and not the servants of others.' Now he looked around the room. 'But the thing that matters most I have not told you. I had been on my own land for two years and I was struggling to survive. There were simply not enough hours to do all that was needful.' He pressed his hands together as though unsure what to say next.

'And so you took someone into your home?' said Blakiston.

King nodded. 'A widow, fifteen years older than me. Her husband was killed by the French in King George's War. She had three sons and two daughters and no means to keep them unless she sold her body.'

There was a sharp intake of breath from Mistress Spence and Lady Isabella looked discomforted. The rector placed his hand on hers.

171

'Mister King, there are subjects that are not suitable…'

'Which, in a sense, she did, for she married me,' King went on as though he had not heard. Then he shook himself. 'I am sorry, Rector, ladies. I have spent too much time alone and my manners were not good at the best of times. Let us speak of other things.'

That would be easier said than done, Blakiston knew. There were things that could not be mentioned in the presence of respectable ladies and those things certainly included the idea that a woman might sell her body. It seemed unlikely that Job King would ever again be invited to dine at the rectory. A coldness hung in the room. To alleviate it, Blakiston said, 'I should like to talk to you, King, about farming methods in America, but I would not inflict on others here a topic so boring. If you have no objection I shall call on you when the wheat harvest is over and we both have more time?'

King nodded. His expression said he was grateful for the diversion.

'Lady Isabella,' said Blakiston, racking his brains for a suitable subject, but he was interrupted. 'Come, come,' said Mistress Spence. 'We are in good company. Mister King, you have raised a subject you should not have raised and I can see that you know it. Lady Isabella and I have lived in the world a while. Are we to see an enjoyable evening spoiled because society would like to believe that we are pampered, protected innocents who must not know what some people have to do? Tell us about life in the colonies. And by that I do not mean, tell us what the ladies there wear.'

At that point, Sarah arrived to help John clear away the soup bowls and carry in the dishes of halibut, roast beef, a stew of chicken and vegetables and steaming bowls of potatoes, cabbage and carrots and the diners lapsed into silence punctuated by quiet murmurs of appreciation. Rosina's skills as a cook were widely spoken of and Blakiston knew that only her liking for and loyalty to Lady Isabella kept her at the rectory in the face of competing offers of higher pay and more servants to order around.

When maid and manservant had finished serving, Sarah had left the room and John had gone to stand once more against the wall, Mistress Spence turned again to Job King. 'The colonies, Mister King.' Blakiston gave silent thanks for a woman so level headed as to have put King's *faux pas* behind her. Had Blakiston still been in the place he had once called home, mixing with the people he had thought of as friends, he knew that the women would have affected a fit of the vapours at hearing the merest suggestion of improper behaviour between men and women. What a generous fate it was that had sent him here, where people talked sense and where he had found to marry a young woman who, he knew, would have taken even less umbrage than had Susanna Spence at what so many would deem an unfitting remark.

'Well,' said King, 'the colonies are not like here. They are rough and they are wild. And yet they are exactly like here, because the first thing you understand when you arrive is that this is another England. But a better England. The people who went from this country to the Americas went, or at least some of them did, because they resented a monarchy and, forgive me, Rector, a church that were very good at spending but themselves produced nothing. They did not leave behind, or at least most of them did not, the ways of kindness and gentleness they had known among their equals here. What they wanted in their new country was to enjoy the rewards of their own work and not to have to feel indebted to those set in place above them.'

Blakiston saw a look of high good humour cross Susanna Spence's face. He had not been in her company before but what was clear was what he had already seen over the matter of Job King's lapse of judgement – a willingness to engage with the world and its people as they really were and not as an outmoded society said they should be. And it was apt, for was this not exactly the virtue that Job King was ascribing to the American colonists? 'What happens,' he asked, 'to those who fall on hard times and cannot support themselves? Does the Poor Law hold in the colonies as well as here?'

'It does, of course, because the colonies are subject to English law. But there is there a level of sharing that we do not see here. When you have a house to build, your neighbours arrive with their tools to help you. Their wives bring food so that no one has to stop the work of construction in order to prepare something to eat. When it is over, they drink, eat, dance and then they leave to go to their own homes. If a man is injured on his land or a woman in childbirth the whole township gathers round to help. And that is true even though a township may cover a huge tract of land with only one or two people to every five square miles.'

'Well, Mr King,' said Lady Isabella, 'you have described a paradise on earth. What was it that led you to leave it all behind and come home?'

'My wife died,' said King. 'If you had asked me at the time we married I would have told you that it was an arrangement of convenience only but I found…no. I am misleading you and I do not want to do that. When my wife died, I was free to come home because she would never have wished to leave America and, if she had, it would not have been to come here. My wife was from Waldeck.' He looked around to make sure that he was being understood. 'And I was rich, or at least rich by the standards of most people there or here, and I had a wish to show people who had known me in my days of poverty what I had made of myself. I know that is a poor ambition and probably unchristian but…'

'It is the most natural thing in the world, sir,' said Susanna Spence. 'What is not usual is your honesty in being so open with us. You are a credit, either to the place that raised you or the one where you made your fortune. But still I wish that you would treat with your labouring men in the same way as others here do.'

'Well,' said King, 'not everyone here deals in the same way with working men. The whole parish is alive with the tale of how Mister Blakiston fed Emmett Batey a breakfast such as that poor man had never seen.'

'Good Lord,' said Blakiston. 'Is everything known in this place?'

'The maid who served you could not contain herself. She said the man was saved from starvation by your kindness. And I believe you gave him tea to drink!'

'Well, you know, small beer is very well but tea is a better drink in the morning. To watch him take it you would think he had never tasted it before.'

'Nor had he, I should think,' said King, 'or at least not legally for the duty the Excise demands puts it beyond the reach of ordinary folk. Most of the tea that is drunk here is smuggled and who knows what matter is mixed with it before it is sold? But your generosity is talked of as though you were Saint Elizabeth of Hungary herself.'

'I had heard nothing of this,' said Lady Isabella. 'I'm sure, Mister Blakiston, that you have earned credit in the world above this one.'

Blakiston was fascinated to see that they had all been so absorbed by the tale that King had to tell that all of the fish and meat courses had been eaten while they listened. Now was the time for another pause while the servants removed the dishes they had wiped clean and brought in two of the puddings Rosina was famous for as well as fruit and the cheese without which the Rector would never consider a dinner to be complete.

Chapter 14

Jeffrey Drabble had told Blakiston that William Snowball was the first person Susannah Ward had seen after finding Margaret Laws dead on the farmhouse floor. Chopwell Garth and New Hope were not the only farms on Lord Ravenshead's estate that were harvesting, had just harvested or were about to harvest and Blakiston was busy each day from early morning till he fell exhausted into bed after a late supper. Almost a week was to pass before he could find time to think once more about the killer of Margaret Laws and Ezra Hindmarsh and it was on Saturday the eighth of September that he went looking for Snowball. Regarded with the caution a squatter must always feel in the presence of a landowner's agent, Blakiston did little to calm the man's fears. He did not wish to spend more time than he must in this sad hovel. It occurred to him, too, that if the other Snowballs did not hear what William Snowball told him they would be less able to align their story with his so he walked out of the single room in which the family lived, slept, cooked and ate and signalled with his head that Snowball should follow him. 'Only you, Snowball. The rest of your family shall remain here.'

When they were outside, Blakiston wasted no time in beginning his attack. 'How did you come to be so close to New Hope Farm that morning?'

'I was looking for a lost pig, Sir.'

'Were you, now? A lost pig. And did you find it?'

'No, Sir.'

'Good grief, man, your very countenance gives the lie to your words. Have you so many pigs, a man like you so poor he must make a beggar's home on common land, that you can afford to let one go? If you had been telling the truth, I and everyone in this parish would have seen you going from door to door searching for your lost treasure. Either that or the air would have been heavy with the smell of roasting pork. Let us put this sad tale behind us; I shall ask you the question once more and this time your answer will be more convincing or you will find yourself in Durham Jail with Joseph Laws. How did you come to be so close to New Hope Farm that morning?'

The hat Snowball turned in his hands looked old enough to have been worn by his grandfather. That could not be, for it was round and in the early years of the eighteenth century when Grandfather Snowball would have been young no-one saw any but three-cornered hats. As Blakiston eyed the grease stains with distaste, he remembered

Drabble's words: "all the Snowballs run to fat". It was true enough in this case, for Snowball was as round as a bee skep and sweat beaded his skin. He looked as though unsure whether to speak or make a run for it but he must have realised that flight would avail him nothing. 'I had heard that Joseph Laws was from home, sir.'

'Indeed. And so you decided to visit New Hope Farm. Was it in expectation of finding something you could purloin? Or did you hope to be yet another having his way with the lady of the house while her husband was elsewhere?'

Snowball looked shocked by the question. His eyes stared wonderingly at Blakiston.

'Come now,' said Blakiston, 'do not waste time dreaming up some new tale that I will see through as easily as the last for you have already shown you are not equipped to lie. Was it his property or his wife you meant to steal from Joseph Laws?'

'Sir, I am a poor man and I have a wife and three children to provide for.'

'Yes, yes, and so you look for possessions others have neglected so that you can take them for yourself. What did you steal?'

'Nothing, Sir. For there was no one in the fields nearby but nor was there anything worth having.'

'How close to the farmhouse did you go?'

It seemed at first that Snowball would be unwilling to answer the question. At length he said, 'To the door itself, Master.'

'To the door! And did you open it?'

'Master, it was already open.'

Blakiston felt a surge of excitement. Had he found someone who had witnessed the evil doings at New Hope Farm? 'And when you opened it, what did you see?'

'Sir, I saw Margaret Laws lying on the floor.' The words were spoken so quietly that Blakiston struggled to be sure he had heard them at all.

'You saw the body? Did you go into the house?'

'Yes, sir, for I did not know then it was a body and I felt the woman might need help. I knew that Joseph Laws had sent Emmett Batey away and I am sore in need of regular work. If I came to his wife's aid I thought he might be grateful enough to offer me employment.'

'He was just as likely to wonder what you were doing in his house at that time. But never mind; when you got close to the woman what was your conclusion?'

'Master, it was clear that she was dead.'

'Dead? Simply that?'

'I saw that she had died at someone's hand.'

'But you did nothing to raise the alarm?'

'No, Master, for I feared I might be blamed for her death.'

'Well, Snowball, that may still happen for there is no-one but you to support your story and you have already shown yourself a man of questionable honesty. What children do you have?'

Snowball appeared bewildered by the sudden change in direction. 'Three girls, Master.'

'Their ages?'

'Nine, seven and two. We lost two more, Master, in the middle. To the diphtheria, you know.'

'Call for the two eldest.' When they were before him, Blakiston addressed them with more gentleness than he had used on their father. 'I want you to run to New Hope Farm and bring Jeffrey Drabble here. Can you do that?'

'Yes, Master,' said the tallest of the two.

Blakiston took three pennies from his purse and handed them to her. 'Good girl. Tell him to come as quickly as he can.'

Blakiston watched the two girls running as fast as their weak and spindly legs would let them. It was a shame to deal with the dispossessed this way and he sometimes felt the weight of the ignominy his class heaped upon those who could not speak up for themselves. Nevertheless, suspicion fell on Snowball and Drabble was needed. He said, 'This is important, Snowball. If you answer truthfully you may help me find Margaret Laws's killer. But if you lie and tell me you saw something you did not see in the hope of removing suspicion from yourself, you will merely increase that suspicion and make it more likely that you will hang. Do you understand?'

Snowball nodded.

'Very well. Think carefully. As you were approaching New Hope Farm and as you were leaving it afterwards, did you see anyone else?'

Snowball stood deep in thought and Blakiston was glad that he had warned him not to invent because he felt sure that the man was considering doing just that. After a long pause, Snowball shook his head. 'No one'.

'You saw no one. Well, I believe you, because it would be in your interest to say that you did. Now think once more. Was there anything that was not as perhaps it should have been? Anything there that should not have been there? Anything not there that should have been there?'

Snowball shook his head again.

'If there was nothing, there was nothing. You said that you had heard that Joseph Laws was from home. How did you hear that? From whom?'

'I cannot remember, Master.'

'Think harder.' A sudden thought came to Blakiston. 'Can you write, Snowball?'

'Write, Sir? No, Sir.'

'You did not write a letter to Joseph Laws? And send it in the post?'

'I cannot write, Master. And if I could, I could not afford the post when I could as easily carry the letter to Joseph Laws and save myself the price. And if it come to that, if I were going to see him then I could tell him what I wanted to say without the trouble of setting it down in writing which I do not know how to do on paper for which I do not have the money.'

'Very well. And here is the constable so your daughters have been speedy about my business. Drabble, William Snowball is under suspicion in the death of Margaret Laws and I wish you to take him in charge.' The same shocked look had returned to Snowball's face and Drabble, too, looked in some doubt. 'Do you think you can manage him without trouble?'

'I can if he comes willingly, Master, but I may struggle if he resists.'

'I see what you mean. Snowball, I instructed you to give more thought to who told you of Joseph Laws's absence.'

The dazed look on Snowball's face intensified at yet another sudden change of direction in the questioning and it occurred to Blakiston that the man was not the brightest among Ryton's inhabitants. 'Master, I...I cannot remember. It was simply something that I heard, I know not where.'

'Then you must go on trying to remember until you succeed. And now we have to deal with the question of how the constable is to take you in charge with no dragoons to support him, since I would be unwilling to accept any assurance from you that you would not run away between here and Durham.'

'Master, if you put me in jail my family will starve. They are starving already but that will be the end of them.'

'Your daughters look skinny enough, it is true. One must wonder how you come to be so fat. Is it at their expense? Do you eat your own portion and that of your family also? Oh, don't trouble yourself with an answer. Here is the solution to our problem. You will go with Drabble now to New Hope Farm and you will work with him on clearing the yard in which the barn stands so that we can begin the task of putting in iron rails before next year's harvest. At night you will sleep in the barn and Drabble will check that you are there at the hours of two and six each morning. How fortunate, Drabble, that you have a watch. If he finds you not there, Snowball, or if you disappear during the day, he will come immediately to tell me and doubt not that we will find you before you have gone far.'

Snowball's expression was brighter than it had been since Blakiston's arrival. 'I will be paid for my work, Master?'

'Nine pence per day. But you need not look so pleased for the money will be given each day to your wife and not to you. Then she may begin to fatten up your children so that they look at last like decent English girls. I have no doubt that Jeffrey Drabble and Dick Jackson will ensure that you do not take more than a fair share of the victuals provided at New Hope. Constable, you do not look happy at my suggestion.'

'I...Master, it is not for me to be happy or unhappy with what you say.'

'You are right. It is not. But there is something on your mind and I will hear it later. For now, get away with him to New Hope, for I have things I must do and tomorrow is a special day for me; I want to be free of all concerns save one.'

Drabble looked down, his face suffused with red, the hat turning in his hands. 'Sir, I do not know whether it is my place to say this or no. But...tomorrow...your banns will be heard for the second time. I think that is why the day is special?'

'It is, Constable.'

187

'Well, sir…sir, I wish to say…sir, I would like to congratulate you on your engagement to Kate Greener.' The final words came out in a rush and Drabble looked away over the fields as though he wished he were somewhere, anywhere, other than here.

Blakiston felt a gentle warmth at the feeling, so clearly genuine, expressed by this rough and unlettered but only too human peasant. 'Thank you, Drabble. I value your words.'

The rest of the day was as busy as Blakiston had anticipated but he went about his business willingly, at least half of his mind always on the happiness he would feel tomorrow. He sank into bed after sending word to the inn that he would take his breakfast at home next morning and not at the inn at Beggar's Bank. Though not vain, he wanted the extra time to take particular care over his appearance. It would be a sorry excuse for a man who could not trouble to look his very best when the woman of his dreams would stand by his side. He had already given instructions that his best linen was to be washed and pressed with exacting attention and the clothes he was to wear on the morrow hung over the backs of chairs in his bedroom.

Next morning he was awake and out of bed long before the necessary time. It was a warm September morning, the sun already over the tops of distant trees, when he stepped into the yard to wash himself carefully under the pump. Then he returned to the house to shave and then to dress. Time passed so slowly that he almost wished he shared the rector's taste for a pipe of tobacco but eventually there came the knock on the door that said breakfast was here. Unusually for him, he wrapped a large linen napkin around his neck and allowed it to fall to his waist so that no dropped food should stain his front. His nervousness about the coming morning was not so great, though, as to inhibit his usual pleasure in the morning repast – indeed, in any meal – and he ate with his customary gusto.

When the serving maid came to collect the large oak board on which his breakfast had been carried in it was still too early to set off for Chopwell Garth and Blakiston chastised himself when he realised that he was taking out his watch at intervals of only three minutes to check whether enough time had passed but eventually it was time to put on his jacket, don his three-cornered hat, lock his door and mount Obsidian. He forced himself to ride to Chopwell Garth at a gentle trot and not the gallop his nervousness urged on him.

Kate had been ready as long as Blakiston had and was waiting with, if anything, more anxiety. When the sound of hooves was heard in the yard, Lizzie told her to sit down. 'Take hold of yourself, man. You don't want to look as though you can't wait to be with him. Stay there and let me open the door and bring him to you.'

Kate pushed past her. 'But I *can't* wait to be with him. And I am not some young girl of the gentry who needs to swoon and seem shy.'

'What will the man think?' said Florrie.

'He knows what he's getting,' Kate answered. 'If he wants to marry me it has to be the me I've always been.' She opened the door and there, less than a foot from her, stood Blakiston. The two simply stared at each other before Blakiston recovered enough to hold out his hand and say, 'Kate. Will you do me the honour of riding to church with me?'

As she took his hand, Kate would have given anything to maintain a calm and dignified exterior but suppressing a giggle proved to be beyond her. She let Blakiston pick her up by the waist and place her on Obsidian's back immediately in front of the saddle before himself vaulting into it and putting his arms around her in order to take the reins.

If she had been asked afterwards what they talked about on the ride to church, Kate could not have answered the question. Conversation she knew there had been but of the subject matter she had no recollection. She would have said, though, that the journey, short as it was, had been among the most contented times of her life.

Contentment was threatened when they reached the church, for Susannah Bent was stepping down from her carriage with her mother and Kate heard the girl's words clearly: 'a spinster on horseback with a man. She's no lady and marriage won't make her one.'

Blakiston leapt from the saddle with a vigour not, perhaps, reflecting the reverence due to arrival at church and wrapped Obsidian's reins round the horizontal post to which three other horses were already tied. He turned to Kate, put his hands once more around her waist, lifted her to the ground and whispered, 'Ignore her'.

When he took her hand in his, keeping her on his left so that he was free to raise his hat to the other church-goers with his right, she gasped at this open expression of affection but her surprise was nothing to that expressed by Susannah Bent. 'Hand holding! And their banns not told three times yet, never mind a marriage gone through! I never saw the like.' Kate glanced at Blakiston and when she saw that he was smothering a laugh she found it impossible to hide her own mirth. They walked into church hand in hand, giggling like two children.

This week, Kate sat in the Estate pew alongside Blakiston and she simply did not care – did not, in fact, notice – how long the rector's sermon went on. She felt herself in heaven and she knew that it was a heaven that smiled on her. And then, the magical moment when Rector Claverley looked at his whole congregation, smiled and spoke the words she was waiting to hear: 'I publish the banns of marriage between James Blakiston, late of Burley parish in the county of Hampshire and now of this parish and Catherine Greener of this parish. This is the second time of asking. If any of you know cause or just impediment why these two persons should not be joined together in holy matrimony, ye are to declare it.' There was no screech from Susannah Bent this time because, immediately before the banns were read, she had risen from her pew and stalked from the church, her face pink and her head held high.

Kate and Blakiston left the church in more orderly fashion after the rector's blessing and engaged in the greetings with other parishioners that went on week after week. Kate had detached her hand from Blakiston's and instead had taken his arm.

Susannah Bent had seen impropriety in all of their actions and Kate and Blakiston had ignored her but some things really could not be done and one of those was for Kate to return, even for a moment, with Blakiston to his house. He therefore put her once again on Obsidian's back and carried her to Chopwell Garth. Even then they risked Society's disapproval because they reached the farm before Tom, Lizzie, Florrie and Lulu and were therefore alone for several minutes. Blakiston stared longingly at the young woman who so captivated him. 'Kate. I should dearly love to kiss you.'

Kate's heart rejoiced. Of course it was wrong for a man and woman who were not married to kiss; Susannah Bent would know that and Society would agree. But Kate was a labourer's daughter and Society foolishness was nothing to do with her. Blakiston wished to kiss her. She wished him to do so. The rector had spoken of impediments when he read their banns and Kate was not entirely sure what an impediment might be but she knew there should be none in this matter. And they had already kissed in the past – once when Blakiston had proposed to her and once on Obsidian's back on the way to New Hope Farm.

She lifted up her face to Blakiston and said, 'I should like you to do so.'

And so, when the Laws family and its offshoots walked into the yard, they found Kate clasped firmly in Blakiston's arms and her lips pressed tight against his. Lizzie coughed. 'Mister Blakiston. Sir. Will you eat dinner with us?'

Kate would have liked nothing more than to hear her love say yes, but she knew the difficulty it would create. 'He has to dine at the rectory tonight. Would you have him look like William Snowball before we are even wed?'

Blakiston smiled. 'It is true, Mistress Laws, that two large meals in one day would be unwise but I should be honoured to share your table if you would permit me to take only a small helping.'

'The honour will be ours,' said Lizzie, 'and you must eat only what you choose.'

'Then I accept your kind offer.'

Kate felt that now the happiness of this day was complete.

Blakiston said, 'There is, though, a condition and that is that you call me James.'

Lizzie looked sad. 'I will with pleasure while you are in our house and at our table, but I beg you not to ask us to do so when we are out or in the company of others.'

'I shall accept that as a small victory but you should know that I will not cease my request until it has been accepted in all places. For are we not to be family?'

When she heard that, Kate had to tear her gaze away from him because she knew that she must look like a beaming idiot. 'Dinner will be some time yet,' she said. 'And I must help in the making. Will you take a seat in the parlour?'

'No,' said Florrie. 'He will not. You have a lifetime ahead of you for seeing to dinners, and it will be shorter than at your age you think. The only thing that never stops is time. Your banns were read for the second time today. The sun is shining. Is your man to sit alone in the parlour while we are all about our business? Go, the two of you, and walk. There will be fewer chances to do that when you are man and wife than you can have any idea of.'

Now it was Blakiston's turn to beam with pleasure. He held out his hand. 'Kate. Will you take my arm?'

And she did, and they walked out of the yard and into the road beyond in a dignified manner that completely failed to hide the pleasure they both felt.

The briar roses in the hedgerow had ceased flowering three months earlier and were now covered in hips that grew more red by the day. Chaffinches and blackbirds sang furiously and the fact that the song was to warn other birds of the presence of human interlopers did not detract from the enjoyment they gave. One of the shire horses that had pulled the harvest carts trotted towards them and put her head over the hedge in the hope that there might be a carrot or an apple on offer. Blakiston squeezed Kate's hand against his side. 'What is in your mind, dear heart?'

Kate pondered the question. What *was* in her mind? She said, 'I cannot quite believe that this is real. That *you* are real. That I did not imagine sitting in church by your side hearing the rector tell everyone that we are to marry. I keep thinking I will wake up and see people laughing at me. Or that I will be walking with you like this and I will look up and see that it is not you but some fat farmer who I dread to spend the rest of my days with.'

'Well,' said Blakiston, 'I confess I understand your concern because *I* wake up in the middle of the night convinced that *I* have been dreaming and that the most wonderful person in my life has *not* consented to become my wife. So what I suggest is that, if it is true and we are both dreaming, we carry on with the dream. And in two weeks' time we will be wed and my life will be better than any dream could ever be.'

Kate laughed and they walked on in silence until she said, 'A little while ago, the whole village was talking about your kindness in giving Emmet Batey a breakfast the like of which he had never eaten. And now, James, the entire parish speaks of William Snowball and the shilling a day his wife receives from you at a time when it is said you think he should be locked up in Durham Jail. You will have beggars knocking at your door asking for help.'

'Batey was hungry through no fault of his own. As for Snowball, the sum is nine pence and not a shilling and I give it to his wife in return for his work to make sure that she and her children are fed. But tell me what you know of Snowball because it was clear when I told Drabble to take him to New Hope that he was reluctant to do so.'

'Well, you are a man who sometimes pretends to be gruff and sometimes makes people believe him but I know that you are the kindest man in Ryton. I do not know why Jeffrey Drabble might not have wanted William Snowball at the farm.'

She was aware of Blakiston's searching gaze. Then he said, 'Kate, forgive me, but I am not sure that you are telling me the whole story. You know

I have seen this before – I saw it when you did not want to say that Margaret Laws was known to be a wanton – and you do it when there is something that, if you told me, would be to someone's disrepute. It is to your credit that you do not like to say something bad about another but I ask you to overcome your discretion and tell me what I need to know.'

Kate sighed. 'No one likes to give William Snowball work. Our Tom says that he works hard and well but he must be watched. It is said that he will take things that are not rightly his.'

'Thank you, Kate. I had already seen something of this but it is good to have it confirmed.'

One of the differences between the class in which working people lived and that of the rector was the time they took their dinner. It was a change that had only come about earlier that century and there were still aristocratic families that took their main meal in the middle of the day but for the most part the moneyed and leisured classes now dined in the evening. Some better-off farmers, seeking to ape the gentry, did the same but Chopwell Garth stuck to the old ways: early in the fields, breakfast at seven in summer and nine in winter, the fields again, dinner in the middle of the day, work once more, a bite to eat brought to them in late afternoon and supper in the kitchen when it was too dark to work out of doors any longer. Sunday mornings were different because they must be in church, but the afternoons were the same.

When Kate and Blakiston returned, Florrie and Lizzie were placing food on the table: a large piece of roast beef; bowls mounded with vegetables of several kinds; a huge jug of gravy that, for all its size, would need to be refilled at least once during the meal. All of this was left on the table and untouched, however, until a soup of vegetables in beef stock had been eaten.

When it was time for the beef, Tom turned to Blakiston. 'Mister Blakiston, will you carve?'

'No, Tom, I will not and not simply because you failed to call me James. This is your house, you are the master of it, this is your table, that is your beef and carving it falls to you. I will thank you to cut for me one slice only.'

Surreptitious smiles were exchanged between Lizzie, Kate and Florrie but Tom turned scarlet as he picked up the knife.

When the beef was eaten and the plates had been cleared away into the scullery, a series of puddings took their place. Kate could never look on this profusion without comparing it to the privations and lack they had known before they had come to the Garth. Truly, life was an amazing thing and even more amazing was the way God worked in it to achieve his ends. If only all could share in the plenty. They were well fed to the point of bursting but she knew that some of their neighbours were close to starvation.

Blakiston took only an apple and Kate knew that soon he must be gone. She told herself to accept what must be but she could not help looking forward to the time two weeks hence when, when Blakiston went home, she would go with him.

And when the moment of separation came, as it had to, Kate walked to the gate and Blakiston walked beside her, leading Obsidian. They stood for a moment, heads almost touching, before Blakiston took her in his arms once more and held her tight. He kissed her – on the forehead, on the cheek, on the throat and, at last, on the lips. Then he rose into the saddle and rode away from Chopwell Garth and Kate returned sadly to the kitchen.

Blakiston's heart was in turmoil as he rode home. He had now kissed Kate four times. Before he had left Hampshire to come here he had been engaged to marry another but her he had never kissed, however he had felt about her and believed she felt about him. It was simply not done in the circles in which he moved.

He shrugged. He knew what people in his Hampshire circle would say: that Kate was no better than she should be; a hussy without respect for herself or the society she moved among. They would be wrong. Since falling in love with Kate, and getting to know her family, he had come face to face with values completely different from those he had grown up with. Different – and more honest. He gave thanks for the fate that had brought him down in the world and transferred him from the soft life he had known to the harder one lived here.

When Blakiston arrived at the rectory that evening, he was greeted by a penitent rector. 'Blakiston. Come into my study. I have something to say that you must hear.'

In the study, Thomas poured two glasses of madeira. Blakiston took his with a smile. His friend was worried; what he was worried about would become clear when the man could spit the words out. At the moment, he seemed to want only to stare through the window. At last, he spun on his heel, determination etched on his face. 'Blakiston. I have a confession to make.'

'A confession? My dear fellow, I give you absolution before I have even heard the words.'

'You will remember the day – that day of my confounded stupidity – the day we fought, here in this very room, over your wish to marry Kate Greener and mine to prevent you? Well, how could you have forgotten?'

'By an act of will, Thomas, for I have put it completely from my mind. I implore you to do the same.'

'I can not until…until I have told you…look here, old man. I wrote to your sister that same day. Immediately you had left here I wrote, such terrible words…but my dear chap, why are you laughing?'

'I *know* you wrote to her. *She* wrote to *me* and told me about it.'

'Oh. Oh, dear. Was she…'

'Apoplectic, my dear fellow. And excruciatingly rude about my choice of bride.'

'I am so sorry.'

'You should not be. You did what you believed to be right.'

'But I have brought dissension into your family.'

'It would have come of its own accord, Thomas. With your help or without it. And now let us speak of something else, for really I never wish to think of these things again.' He remembered the question that had come into his head several times since he had first heard Thomas read his banns. 'Tell me. When you ask for cause or just impediment why two people should not be married, does anyone ever answer?'

'Oh, my dear fellow. If only you had heard some of the things that I have heard. The man who objected when he saw that the dowry he had hoped a young woman would bring him was to go to another. It was the money he wanted and not the woman. The sweet-faced, seemingly innocent young maid who became a screaming harridan when she heard that the rogue whose child she carried had betrothed himself to another. The man whose banns we had already published twice and were to do so for the third and final Sunday when two women I had never seen before, with five children between them, took their seats at the very back of the church before the service began. I knew something was afoot for they were veiled and they took care that neither their own faces nor those of their children could be seen but I had no idea what they intended. We went all the way through the service and then when I said, "If any of you know cause or just impediment why these two persons should not be joined together in holy matrimony, ye are to declare it", these two stood as one, doffed their veils and in unison announced, "The just impediment is that he is already married". Then, in turn, they pointed a finger at themselves and said, "To me!"

'Good Heavens! What happened?'

'It became clear that the would-be groom was in the habit of marrying women of substance – they were both widows, James, as was the putative bride from our own parish – and absconding with their dowries. He was arrested but on the way to Durham Jail he disappeared. I am sure he gave money to the Captain of Dragoons but there was no way to prove it. In any case, we never saw him again. But that is the maid tapping on the door to tell us dinner is ready. Shall we go in?'

Chapter 15

At six next morning, Jeffrey Drabble and William Snowball began the work of preparing the harvested fields for gleaning. By nine, the lane beyond the hedges had already been filled for two hours by jostling parishioners and their children anxious to gather up every scrap of usable grain that the reapers had left. The two men opened the gate to let the crowd in and walked back to New Hope Farm for breakfast. Dick Jackson, who had been at Gaskell Lodge carrying out the same work for Job King, joined them.

Drabble was glad that Dick was here, for the unease he always felt in Snowball's presence had not abated. Susannah Ward moved round the table, pouring small beer for all three men and setting out butter, ham, cheese and a loaf of bread. Dick was hacking off a slice of the cheese to put on the bread he had already cut for himself when the maid came back with a flat black frying pan in which sizzled a wide and thick yellow confection. 'What's this?' he demanded.

'It's eggs, you stupid old man,' said Susannah. 'What do you think it is?'

'There's no need to speak to me like that, woman. You should treat your elders with more respect.'

'Yes,' said Drabble. 'Dick knew your mother before you were born.' He put his hand to his chin. 'Now there's a thought. How old are you, Susannah Ward?'

Dick laughed but Susannah looked furious. 'Dick Jackson is no father of mine and if you talk about my mother like that I'll break your head with this skillet.'

'Be that as it may,' said Drabble, 'the dish surprised us.'

'We have a lot of eggs,' said Susannah, 'and no one is taking them to market. Better to eat them, I thought, than let them go to waste. I'll think differently next time.'

William Snowball had carved himself a big chunk of the cooked eggs and was tucking in with evident pleasure. 'Don't do that, pet. This is lovely.'

'Rosina at the rectory told me how to make it. It's French. She called it an amlet. And don't you call me pet,' said Susannah.

'French?' said Dick, putting down his knife.

'If you don't want it you don't have to eat it.'

When she had flounced out, Snowball said, 'Did they not offer you breakfast at Gaskell Lodge, Dick Jackson?'

'They did. But there is no more work for me there until Thursday and so I came back here for the pleasure of making Susannah Ward cross. Don't eat the whole of that egg thing, William Snowball; leave some for me and Jeffrey Drabble.'

'You're going to eat it then? Even though it's French? I wonder what American breakfasts are eaten at Gaskell Lodge?'

'Job King feeds his men on the same things that we eat here.'

Drabble had been aware for some time of Snowball's watery eyes on him. He cut himself a slice of amlet and stared at the other man. 'I think you have something you want to say.'

'Yes,' said Snowball.

Drabble waited but it seemed that Snowball was having difficulty in going further. 'Out with it then.'

'I think you have the ear of Mister Blakiston. I believe he listens to what you say.'

So that was it, Drabble thought. He wants employment and he imagines that I, who have no position and am hired by the day just as he is, can help him get it. Well, let him ask. I'll not speak the words for him. He turned to Dick Jackson. 'You should eat this. I know how you feel about the French after you were there in the wars but this is good. Try a bit.'

'Well, I will,' said Dick. 'I'd best be quick or yon greedy bugger will have had the lot.' He picked up his knife and removed the remaining omelette from the pan.

'Well, will you or won't you?' said Snowball.

Drabble turn to look at him. 'Will I what? You have not asked me to do anything.'

Snowball mopped what was left of his egg with a piece of bread. 'Help me with Blakiston,' he said. 'What were we talking about?'

'I am a day labourer. The same as you. Do you not think I would help myself, and Dick Jackson here, before you?'

'You are old men,' said Snowball. 'And you have no families. No children to feed. No wife to nag you when you have no money.' He leaned across the table. 'Look, Jeffrey Drabble, I know what it is that troubles you. But now you have seen me here at the harvest and, whatever else you may think, you know I am a hard worker. Do you not?'

'Aye,' said Drabble. 'I will not deny you that. You have worked as hard as any man I have known.'

'And as well,' said Snowball.

Drabble nodded. 'As hard and as well. It is true.'

'So?'

Drabble cut himself more bread and cheese to eat with his omelette. 'We should be nicer to yon maid. There are few who cook this well and even fewer who will do so for the likes of us. Jemmy Rayne will be a lucky man when he weds her.'

'Yes,' said Snowball, 'you are right, she treats us well considering what an ill-tempered wench she is and we would do well to treat her the same. But we were speaking of me.'

Drabble slammed down his knife. 'No. *You* were speaking of you. I was trying to avoid it. Yes, it is true, you are a hard worker. It is also true that you are known as a man who cannot tell the difference between what is his and what belongs to others. You were the first person to find Margaret Laws dead in this place and if you told us the truth about that, which as we all know is something you find difficult to do, you would not say that you were worried about a farmer's wife. You were here because you hoped to find something that was not yours that you could use or sell.'

He picked up his knife and angrily speared a piece of cheese. He was aware of three pairs of eyes on him. Dick Jackson was smiling calmly in that way he had as he observed the world around him. Susannah Ward stood in the doorway watching Drabble and drinking in every word. And William Snowball had turned white and was clutching his knife in a tense fist. 'You had better put that knife down,' said Drabble, 'for I promise you, you are watched with interest. Do you deny what I have said?'

Snowball did not answer. Instead, he forced as much food into his mouth as it was possible for one mouth to hold, raised himself from his bench, broke wind loudly and marched out of the kitchen, slamming the door behind him.

Dick Jackson held up his pot. 'Susannah Ward, your beer is as good as your amlet. Do you have more of either?'

The maid stepped forward and served beer from her jug. 'The amlet is all done. I am happy you enjoyed it. If no one comes to take the eggs to market, I will cook another tomorrow.'

Jackson sipped at his beer. 'You have made yourself an enemy, Jeffrey.'

'I would rather have William Snowball as an enemy than as a friend. You have never told me – not really *told* me – what it was like in France.'

Dick's smile faded. 'This is a strange conversation. We were talking about Snowball and suddenly you speak of France.'

'Ever since you returned it seems that you find the world an amusing place. Whatever bad things happen, they do not trouble you as they trouble others. What happened to you there, to make everything now a reason to smile?'

'You are right. I do not speak of it. And if I did, you would not thank me. Susannah Ward, that was the best breakfast I have eaten in a long time. If Jemmy Rayne finds another, you may apply to me with every confidence of acceptance as my wife.'

'Hah! I would as soon be chained to a Musselman as to an old goat like you.'

'She is right,' said Drabble. 'I do not think, at our age, we could hope to keep so hearty a maid happy for long.'

'That is no business of either of you,' said the maid. 'And now, find somewhere else to be for I have work to do in this kitchen.'

While the labouring men had been readying the harvested fields for gleaning and then taking breakfast, Blakiston had been on his way to the Durham County Gaol. He was aware that the only suspect he had for the murder of Margaret Laws was Margaret's husband, Joseph. While Blakiston had serious doubts about Joseph's guilt, there were questions the man must answer before he could go free.

He did not see the gaol as a safe place for Obsidian and therefore gave the ostler at The Turk's Head three pence to stable the horse before walking to Saddler Street. There an obstacle presented itself when the gaoler demanded that Blakiston hand over his pistols before entering. 'You are mad,' said Blakiston. 'Or you believe I am. You expect me to walk into this home of thieves and villainous cutpurses without the means to defend myself?'

'That is the rule I am given,' said the gaoler. 'No one may visit a prisoner armed. I should have prevented it the first time you were here. I could lose my position.'

'You could lose your life if you attempted to enforce such a foolish regulation.' Blakiston handed him two pence. 'Find a room where I can sit without being overcome by filth and damp, difficult though that may be in such a hovel. Then bring the prisoner to me and fetch him a cup of small beer. You may spend what is left on a drink for yourself. And let us hear no more about the giving up of pistols.'

The money was clearly enough to settle the man's conscience and soon Blakiston and Joseph Laws were sat together in a room that was at least dry, though cleanliness was beyond the gaoler's ability to provide. 'Laws,' said Blakiston, 'it is time for you to tell the truth. You say you did not kill your wife and I am inclined to believe you for there has been another killing of a very similar nature which you could not have performed because you were locked up here at the time. Nevertheless, you are the first and only suspect for Margaret's murder and unless you talk to me in a way that makes me understand your actions you will swing for it after the next assize. Do you understand what I am saying to you?'

Joseph Laws licked his lips and nodded.

'Your wife's body bore signs of beating. And more than once. I believe that it was you who assaulted her. Do you deny that?'

Laws shook his head.

'Why did you beat her?'

Laws looked at his feet. 'Mr Blakiston, let me congratulate you on your engagement to Kate Greener for I never had the chance to do so when your banns were called. You have chosen well. That is something I could not do for I wanted to be sure of Home Farm and I took the only bride available to me. I paid a heavy price for that farm.'

He fell silent and eventually Blakiston realised that he would have to point out that what he had heard was not enough. 'A heavy price?'

'My wife was born to be a whore. No normal marriage and no normal man could ever have been enough for her.'

'You discharged your serving man, Emmett Batey.'

'I came from the fields and found him with Margaret, doing what they should not have been doing. If I had not driven him immediately from the farm I would have killed him. But he was not the only one.'

A melancholy entered Blakiston's heart. He knew that Laws was right when he said that he, Blakiston, had chosen his bride well and it saddened him to know that unhappiness such as Laws had known could exist between man and woman. 'There is no need to go on. I do not need to hear the full list. And I have pity for you. But you must see that this does not help your position. If your wife manoeuvred to get you out of the house and, indeed, out of the county on the night that your maid was also from home in order to satisfy her lust with some other man, your anger on returning home would be ample reason for murder. I imagine her behaviour would see a sentence of hanging commuted but you would still be a likely candidate for transportation to the colonies.'

'I don't know that it was Margaret who sent that letter. I don't know that she saw a man while I was away.'

'That is not what happened? You did not return home to find a man with her?'

Laws shook his head. 'What happened is what I told you happened. I came home and she was already dead.'

'And you saw no-one.'

'No-one.'

'Well, it is unhelpful. For when there is a victim the law will require an antagonist and there is no-one but you.'

Laws shivered. 'I feel the hemp on my neck already. But you said there had been another killing. Who?'

When Blakiston had told him the story of Ezra Hindmarsh, Laws shook his head. 'My wife. Someone else's child. There is no pattern to this, Mister Blakiston. There is a madman loose, who kills without reason wherever he sees the chance.'

There was no more to be done here, and Blakiston called the gaoler to take Laws back to his cell. The relief of once more breathing the untainted air of the Durham streets was tempered by two thoughts: that Joseph Laws might hang for a murder someone else had committed; and that, if Laws were correct and the murders had been carried out without pattern or motive, there was no knowing how many more would die unless he found the killer. And how was he to find someone who killed for no reason?

Then a third thought nagged at him and he turned back and tugged on the rope beside the gaol door. Door and walls were thick, but he could hear the bell tolling inside and he kept ringing until the gaoler's bad-tempered face appeared in the doorway. 'What visitors has Joseph Laws had besides me?'

'Him? He has had none.' The gaoler moved to close the door and Blakiston used his foot to prevent it. 'He congratulated me on my engaging to marry. But he was already in here when the banns were first rung. Who told him of it?'

Contempt played across the gaoler's face. 'There are people in and out of here all the time, overseer. If someone thought your affairs worth speaking of, someone else will have heard and talked of it. And now I'll thank you to remove your boot from my door and let me be about my business.'

The life of Lord Ravenshead's agent was a busy one and Blakiston had five farms to visit that Monday. Coming from Durham City meant that he entered His Lordship's domain from the side furthest from Chopwell Garth and Home Farm and he began his inspection at the farm nearest to hand. It was three in the afternoon when he reached Home Farm. Jeffrey Drabble was at work in the yard repairing damage suffered by one of the carts used in the harvest. Dick Jackson was helping him. Of William Snowball there was no sign.

Blakiston tied Obsidian to a post close enough to the drinking trough to let the horse quench his thirst. 'You had trouble with the cart?'

'They are not so sturdy as waggons,' said Jackson.

'Perhaps not,' said Blakiston, 'but they make the work quicker and easier. Do they not, Dick Jackson?'

Challenged in this way, Dick could only acknowledge that what the overseer said was true. A man was more content if things remained as they had been in his father's and his grandfather's day but life was not like that. You had only to look at the way the coal pits were growing, and the villages for the men that worked them, and the manufactories in towns like Newcastle and Darlington that were so much bigger than anything that had existed when he was a boy. Not that he went to Newcastle or Darlington any more. In any case, whatever he might think, carts were replacing wagons and they had better get on with repairing this one.

'Where is William Snowball?' asked Blakiston.

'Gone off in a tiff,' said Drabble. 'Though he will know that you are here and as he wishes to speak to you doubt not that he will return.'

And he was right, for at that very moment Snowball entered the yard. His face still bore signs of the rage in which he had departed.

'Jeffrey Drabble tells me you are in a tiff, William Snowball. About what? He also says you wish to speak to me and I ask again: about what?'

Snowball could not be unaware that there was nothing welcoming about Blakiston's questions and the agent watched his face grew redder. 'Mr Blakiston, it is not easy for a working man to raise a family when he does not know from one day to the next whether he will be employed. I asked Jeffrey Drabble to speak to you on my behalf but he would not and so I must ask you myself. I have shown in this harvest how hard and how well I can work. Can you offer me a permanent place?'

'We have not yet decided what to do about Home Farm. It may remain as it is with a new farmer or I may join it with Chopwell Garth. The farmer of course will not be you and as for labourers, Emmett Batey has first call here.'

'But he left!' said Snowball.

'And he is to return,' said Blakiston. 'That is my decision to make and I have made it. Dick Jackson, is it your impression that Job King has room for another labourer?'

'He is certainly more ready than farmers hereabouts to care about those in need.'

'Not surprising, since he was one of us before he went to the Americas,' said Drabble.

'Well, then,' said Blakiston, 'I suggest, Snowball, that you address yourself to Mr King.'

'Mr Blakiston,' said Snowball, 'would you speak to him on my behalf?'

Blakiston could think of no reason why he should offer assistance to a man he did not care for but on the other hand he could think of no reason why he should not. Life was hard for labouring men and it was easy – too easy – to ignore hardship simply because there was so much of it all around him. 'I will see what he has to say on the matter.'

'Thank you, Sir.'

'And now, help Jeffrey Drabble and Dick Jackson make good this cart. When that is done, carry out whatever other work the constable directs you to do. And let me hear no more of tiffs and bad temper.'

Chapter 16

It was early evening when Blakiston reached home and the warmth of the sun made him regret that he had but a small yard and no spacious garden, such as he had enjoyed in his childhood home, in which to relax and simply enjoy the peace. As was his custom, he stabled Obsidian and prepared to walk across the road to the inn to take his supper. The horse's need to feed came before his own and while he was seeing to this a man he did not recognise left the spot where he had been resting in the shade of the village cross, doffed his round hat and stood in a manner that indicated he wished permission to speak. The man's livery suggested that he was in service but Blakiston did not recall seeing him in any of the houses in which he had dined.

'You are?'

'Sir, I am Mister King's man.'

'Yes? You wish to speak to me?'

'Sir, Mister King wishes to know if you will do him the honour of dining with him tomorrow at six of the evening?'

Blakiston considered the invitation. 'I believe Gaskell Lodge has a handsome garden?'

'It has, Sir.'

'Then please tell Mister King that I shall be pleased to accept his invitation.' The man hesitated and Blakiston said, 'You have something else to say?'

'Sir. You see to the stabling of your own horse? Have you no man of your own?'

'No, and no need.'

'Sir, I have a younger brother…'

'I am very pleased for you, but so long as I am single I do not need the attentions of a servant. When I am married, things will be different, but choosing a servant then will be a task for my wife and not me. Now be about your business.'

As he crossed the road, he thought about what he had just said. It was true; Kate would need her own staff – at the very least, a maid to do the heavy work involved in keeping the place clean and more than that when children began to arrive – and it was something they had not discussed. He had better see that they did so for today was Monday, their banns would be called for the last time on Sunday and the week after that they would be wed.

The inn was a simple place. It catered for people passing through and single men like Blakiston who had enough income to eat there and no cook of their own. There was a public room in which the poorer men of the parish (women were rarely seen there other than as serving maids) could enjoy a penny pint of ale brewed on the premises, and a comfortable saloon in which the more solvent ate. The innkeeper's wife was known for keeping a clean house and they employed a gardener whose duties mostly involved raising vegetables for the kitchen and hops for the brewhouse.

The food was, in general, as simple as the inn and Blakiston found it none the worse for that. The centrepiece of tonight's meal was a rabbit pudding in which chunks of meat were joined with pieces of carrot and turnip in a thick and tasty gravy. When the innkeeper stopped by his table to fill his mug with beer he asked, 'Are you enjoying the pudding, Mister Blakiston?'

'Delicious. You know, where I lived before I came here, this rabbit would have been baked in a pie for I rarely saw puddings until I journeyed north. I must say, your cook has an excellent way with the pudding.'

'As good as Rosina's at the rectory, that we hear so much about?'

'Ah, now, there are few as good as hers. But this is most enjoyable in its own right.'

Next day, Blakiston took care to finish his round of farms in time to get home, wash his face at the pump and change his clothes before once again getting on Obsidian's back and riding to Gaskell Lodge where the horse was taken into the house's own stable. Job King came out to greet him. 'Mister Blakiston, I am so glad you felt able to take up my invitation for you wished to speak of farming as it is conducted in the colonies and we did not have the chance to talk about that. But James tells me that you have an interest in the garden. We have a shady bower close to the house. Would you like to eat there?'

'I should like that very much, Mister King.'

'Then let us take our seats and I shall call for wine. Or would you like beer?'

'Whatever you prefer, I shall join you in it.'

What King had called a bower, Blakiston knew as an arbour. A seat large enough for four wide behinds was surrounded at the back and on both sides by a rose that rambled over a wooden trellis. While King was in the house giving his instructions, Blakiston listened to the birds; their calls may have sounded like idle chatter but he knew that in fact they were warning of the interloper. The scent of roses hung on the air. When King bustled back into the garden, he was followed by servants: men carrying a table and maids with glasses and bottles of red wine. King took charge of the pouring, before raising his glass to Blakiston. 'Sir, your health.'

'And yours, too, Mister King.'

Dinner at Gaskell Lodge was rather more elaborate than the pudding Blakiston had eaten at the inn the previous evening, for there were proprieties to be observed in entertaining guests and King was aware of them. A number of servants waited on them and Blakiston knew that King could not have so many house servants. Indeed, their style of dress made it clear that those who had carried the table were more regularly employed in the gardens or on the farm. Whatever their regular work, the serving men and women stood well back so that they could not hear what was being said at the table but could be called by a beckoning finger at any moment.

Blakiston was struck by the difference between King's behaviour and what happened elsewhere. The custom at the rectory was the same as it had been in his Sussex home while he was growing up – servants were invisible and no one cared what they might hear. When he thought of it in these terms he felt shame, but it was a fact that the lower classes were not noticed by the circles in which he moved. Blakiston realised that it would never be possible for Kate to treat servants that way; for Job

King, too, it could not be, for King would recognise these people as his own. In fact…Blakiston looked closely at the footman who had brought him here. 'That man…is he…?'

King smiled. 'His father was my father's brother.'

'I see. And the serving maid at the far end?'

'His sister.'

'I do see. So you prefer to have your own kin about you?'

'It is not a matter of preference, Mister Blakiston. Times are hard, people starve and I do not wish any more of those who are close to me to be among them.'

'Any more?'

'My family has suffered too many deaths. It is one thing when the diphtheria comes or the influenza or when a man gets between a she-bear and her cub, which is how one of my neighbours in the colonies died. There is no escape from disease or the fury of an animal. But starvation is a different matter. When you watch someone fade away and die, a thing that takes months, for no cause but that they have not enough to eat – that is almost as painful for the watcher as for the watched. You may never have been that watcher. But I have.'

'And that is why you went to Virginia?'

'It was that or change from watcher to watched. Become one more who wasted away to skin and bone and ended in the churchyard. But enough. I did not invite you here to listen to tales of sadness. Let us try the soup.' And he lifted a hand to signal that service should begin. 'And my dear man, I have allowed you to sit with an empty glass. What sort of host will you think me?'

The soup was good. When it was finished, bowls and tureens were cleared away and then the table was spread with dishes – salads, vegetables, roast chicken, boiled beef, fish and a selection of sweet things. Blakiston fell to with a will. 'Your cook. Is she, too, a family member?'

'No, Mister Blakiston, for I would not take risks with the quality of the food I am served. I kept on the cook who was here before.'

'But you rent the house? You have not bought it?'

'When I arrived I was not sure whether I would stay or return to the colonies. And so I came to an arrangement to rent for twelve months at the end of which, if I stay, the rent I have paid will be set against the purchase price.'

'And will you? Stay?'

King put down his knife, a thoughtful look on his face. 'No,' he said at last. 'When I came here, I thought I should probably end my days in the place where they had begun. But now…I believe Virginia is the right home for me.'

'Because…?' Unlike King, Blakiston had not stopped eating during this conversation. He was enjoying the meal too much. The food was as good as he had had anywhere and the pleasure of eating outdoors as great as he had expected.

Perhaps encouraged by Blakiston's obvious enjoyment, King returned to his meal. 'I think I was there too long. I am more American now than I am English. I can never be as comfortable here as I was there.'

'And yet you said, when we dined at the rectory, that the colonies were simply England removed.'

'Yes, and that is true. But it is England with a difference. People do not speak there of nobles and the middling classes and the mass of common working people, and nor are those common people held in scorn by people who think themselves their betters. Our rulers believe they can maintain in the colonies the same abject submission they expect here and they are wrong. There is trouble coming, Mister Blakiston. And when it comes I would rather be with the colonists.'

'But surely…the British Army…you do not suggest that a bunch of farmers can stand against that?'

'Well, we shall see. But do not imagine it was the redcoats alone who defeated the French in the recent wars. Without the settlers they could not have done it. Our leaders do many stupid things but one of the stupidest was to reject Washington.'

'Washington? I have not heard the name. I believe there is a place called Washington not far from here.'

'That may be where the family went to Virginia from but they have been there a hundred years or more. George Washington is a big man. He hunts on horseback in a red coat, like any English squire, which is how I think he sees himself. He owns several thousand acres and keeps more servants than anyone hereabouts, not excluding the Blacketts or Lord Ravenshead. He is a slave owner, too. But what I am talking about is his military prowess. He fought as a Colonel in General Braddock's army against the French. He helped the British capture Fort Duquesne and win control of the Ohio Valley. But when he asked for a commission in the British Army, they laughed at him. That ridicule may return to haunt them.'

'You believe trouble is likely, then?'

King topped up Blakiston's wineglass once more. 'If the government here fails to understand the feelings of people there, we shall have war. If they continue to insist that colonists shall have no say in how they are governed, we shall have war. It will be civil war, the very worst kind. Englishman against Englishman. I dread it. But if it must be, I had rather be with those Englishmen over there than with their countrymen here.'

'And your kinsfolk who work for you at Gaskell Lodge? You will leave them once more to the tender mercies of the better off?'

'They will go with me. Not, as I did, to be indentured at the end of a free passage. No, I will pay their fares and they will travel with me. It will not be comfortable, for crossing the Atlantic is never comfortable, but when we reach the Susquehanna River they will see that the journey was worth the making.'

As Blakiston rode home, it occurred to him that the object of the meeting had been for him to learn something about colonial farming practices and that these had not been mentioned, so absorbing had the conversation on other matters been.

Some time ago, he had reflected on the unlikely circumstances that had brought Tom Laws to the position of farmer instead of labourer and he had wondered how many more of those raised in poverty could do well if only the opportunity were offered. Now here in Job King he had another example. For the country to thrive, it surely needed to make maximum use of the capabilities of all its people. As, to listen to Job King, the colonies were doing.

But he had better stop thinking this way, for in the reign of King George it was probably treasonous even to entertain such thoughts.

Next day was Wednesday and after breakfast Blakiston saddled Obsidian and rode to Chopwell Garth. Kate met him with a smile and, as he always did, he found himself smiling automatically in return. 'Kate. My love.'

'James. Is it Tom you are here to see? Or me?'

'I shall see Tom Laws before I leave, but my business is with you. A maid.'

Kate's smile became broader. She knew what Blakiston was about to say but saw no harm in teasing him a little. 'Yes, James, I am still a maid. In two weeks or so, you will have the church's blessing to alter that. And mine, too. James, you have gone bright red.'

'No, no…I mean, you will need a maid when we are wed.'

'Do you think so? Your house is not large. There will only be the two of us to look after. I am used to harder work than that.'

'Please, Kate, do not be difficult. You will need a maid. You must have one. It should be someone of your choosing.'

'Well, of course I have known that this conversation was coming. Do you remember when I told you about Rosie Miller?'

'I do. It was at the rector's tithing party, when I was still looking for the killer of Reuben Cooper. I was about to send Jemmy Rayne to make enquiries in Staithes.'

'But I am not allowed to know that.'

'But you are not allowed to know that. It was also that sad time when I had not yet declared my love for you…'

'…and I had come to believe that you never would.'

'You told me that Rosie Miller had gone to work in the kitchens at Matfen Hall and that you feared for her safety at the hands of the Blackett men.'

'I should like to ask Rosie if she would come to work for us as our maid. She may not wish to, because she was my friend when both of us were poor and…well. I'm sure you understand.'

'I do. She might not be happy taking orders from someone who was once her friend.'

'And, I hope, still is, whatever differences there will be in our life. But if she will…if she says yes…then she will be safe from the Blacketts. Our mam says that Mary Stone was a sweet girl just like Rosie until the Blacketts got hold of her, and you know how she turned out.' She peered up at Blakiston from beneath the brim of her cap.

'Why are you smiling like that?'

'Mistress Wortley told me that I should never say Our Mam. And I do not. I said it to tease you and to remind you that the girl you are about to wed is not worthy of you.'

'Really, Kate, you do talk nonsense sometimes. It is I who am not worthy of you.'

'Yes, well, we could spend the next two days each saying to the other, no, no, it is me; I am the one who is not worthy. In any case, how do you feel about Rosie Miller as our maid?'

'If she is who you want, she is who I should like you to have. How will you get word to her? For I confess I do not wish to be anywhere near Sir Edward Blackett.'

'I have wanted to ask you about that, James. Is it true that he offered you marriage with one of his family? And a home and money to go with it?'

'Good God! Does everyone know everything about everyone else's business in this place?'

'So it is true. Why did you refuse his offer?'

'For the same reason, I should think, as you rejected the stream of farmers asking for your hand. I wished to marry for love. As I shall do the week after next. But I asked you a question.'

'That will be easy. Her mother is here, still close to where I lived not so long ago. I shall ask her to get a message to Rosie. And now that we have settled that, would you like to wait for Tom? He has been in the fields three hours now and will soon be here for breakfast.'

Blakiston did not, in fact, have any pressing business with Tom and the reason he allowed himself to be shown into the kitchen was that time at Chopwell Garth was time in the presence of the young woman he loved. When Lizzie attempted to move him into the parlour, Blakiston said, 'Parlours are for ceremony. Kitchens are for family. I should like you to think of me as a kitchen person.' He could not fail to see the doubt in the way Lizzie looked at him and he smiled in response.

Little Louise, kept safe by an arrangement of wooden bars, was grizzling quietly and Kate picked her up and plopped her down on Blakiston's lap. Blakiston, who had never held a baby in his life, rushed to place his hands around her before she should fall. The grizzling stopped and two eyes, grey as was normal among the Greeners, stared upwards at this face she had not seen so close before. Tiny hands reached up towards him. Mesmerised, Blakiston lifted the child with great care. A surge of love possessed him when the little hands began to pat his face.

He was aware of three pairs of eyes on him. Kate's expression radiated uncertainty about what she had done in placing a babe so casually into the care of a man – and a member of the gentry at that. On Lizzie's face he could see conflict between worry over Louise's safety and a desire to laugh. Florrie, on the other hand, showed nothing but concern at the way their guest had been treated.

And then it was over, for Tom came through the door, Louise turned and reached out towards him and a flustered Tom plucked his daughter from Blakiston's arms.

Blakiston smiled because he must, but his mind was in turmoil. Kate no doubt believed that the children she hoped to give him would be the first he had. He wished that that were true. Before he had left Hampshire to come here, before his father had lost what should have been his inheritance, when he was but twenty years old, Blakiston had fathered a child on a young woman and failed to honour his obligation to make an honest woman of her. The rector knew this story because it had come out when Blakiston was investigating the murder of Reuben Cooper, but Kate did not. A voice inside his head said that it was long ago, that he had been a different person, that his love for Kate had transformed him and that he did not need to tell her. Another voice disputed this.

The women in the room interpreted his sudden silence as embarrassment over the holding of a child. He was content for the moment to let them think that.

'Mister Blakiston,' said Lizzie.

'Elizabeth Laws, you promised to call me James in the privacy of this house.'

Lizzie's face turned bright red. 'James. Will you eat breakfast with us?'

'I breakfasted before I left home this morning. But I will take a dish of tea with pleasure.'

Florrie and Kate had been moving back and forth between scullery, pantry and kitchen and now on the table stood fried black pudding, bacon, bread, butter and an egg dish that, had they but known it, closely resembled the amlet that Susannah Ward had served to the labourers at New Hope Farm. Blakiston drank his tea and watched the earnestness with which Tom and Ned after three hours in the fields attacked the food before them. He gave no sign of the torment in his head. A bastardy bond had made him responsible for the upkeep of his illegitimate son should he ever become a charge on his home parish. It was now three years since he had been asked for money. That meant that something had happened to relieve the parish of the need to support the boy – but what? Had he died? Had his mother found someone to marry and support her? For it was sure that she had no skill that would enable her to maintain herself and a child. Blakiston felt a deep shame. The voice that had said there was no reason for Kate to know was wrong. If he married her without telling her what he had done, he would be keeping from her something she needed to know.

'Mister Blakiston,' said Tom. 'Is Joseph to be tried for murdering his wife?'

Blakiston knew there was no point in asking Tom to call him James, as he had asked Lizzie, and it was probably as well given their master-servant roles. He also understood that it was natural that Tom should ask this question. But the fact was that he had little information to give. He said, 'Your brother is guilty of something, Tom. Why else would he have attacked me and run off? If you want my opinion, he did not murder Margaret Laws. But he need not be charged or released until it is time for the next Assize and that is many months away.'

'He is held in an awful place,' said Tom.

'Yes, he is and he would not be had he not attempted to brain me with an iron pot.'

'Would it be all right if I were to visit him in prison?'

'Of course it would. You may do so whenever you wish, though you had better take care – there are footpads between here and Durham. And when you get there, you will find the jailer a most unpleasant person.'

'You could take Joseph a change of clothes,' said Florrie.

'And some food,' said Kate.

'Yes, you could, but make sure that you do not part with them until you have placed them in Joseph's hands. That place is a den of thieves and I do not exclude the jailer.'

When it was time for Blakiston to go, Kate walked with him to where Obsidian waited in the shade. 'Are you going to tell me?' she asked. Blakiston looked at her without speaking. 'Something has been worrying you,' she went on. 'What is it?'

'Am I so easily understood?'

'Not by everyone, perhaps. But I have come to know you. There is something that you think I should know that you do not want to tell me. I think you must be afraid that I would not like it.' She stopped speaking and stared into his eyes. The challenge was obvious and he accepted it. He told

Kate the story he did not want to tell her – the story of which he was so ashamed.

When he was done, there was silence between them. Blakiston did not speak because he could not think of a single thing to say and Kate's face said that she was struggling with emotion. Blakiston feared that he was to regret his honesty.

Then, quietly, Kate said, 'Thank you for telling me. It cannot have been easy.'

'You are not going to cast me off?'

'Oh, James. What you have just shown is how right I was to accept you. You did something that was wrong. You know you did. The world is full of people who do things that are wrong and never accept that they did, even to themselves.' She placed her hands flat on his chest. 'You are a good man. And I am very lucky.'

Blakiston rode away lighter in spirit than he had been a little earlier.

Chapter 17

He thought about what he was about to do, and the thoughts were not good. He had been driven to this and he had had no doubts about the rightness of what he was doing. He kept it to himself because, in the society he lived in, that was the sensible thing to do – but he was no believer. He had not believed since he was a small child in the things the Bible had to say. Nevertheless, it was all there. *And thine eye shall not pity, but life should go for life, eye for eye, tooth for tooth, hand for hand, foot for foot.* And that had been his guiding principle. An eye for an eye and a life for a life. That's what he had set out to do. It had seemed right. It seemed right no longer. There were other words that he could recall from long hours on hard pews. *Ye have heard that it hath been said, An eye for an eye, and a tooth for a tooth. But I say unto you, that ye resist not evil: but whosoever shall smite thee on thy right cheek, turn to him the other also.* None of it meant anything to him, because he was long past the point where biblical words could relieve his hurt. And he owed it, did he not, to those of his who were dead? Had they received compassion? They had not.

Had Walter Maughan known pain because of the death of his daughter? If he had, he kept it well hidden. But what about Ezra Hindmarsh? His hurt was palpable. Yes, Ezra Hindmarsh had been responsible for the deaths he mourned. Yes, it was right that Ezra Hindmarsh should pay the price. And yet...

The misery enjoyed by Ezra Hindmarsh was hard to watch. He had expected to enjoy seeing others suffering from the pain that had once been inflicted on him. He had thought that this would be a catharsis – a working out of his own pain in the pain suffered by others.

And it wasn't true. Old Ezra Hindmarsh suffered – and so did he. He would have needed a heart of stone to see the old man's pain and not to be moved by it. Which was odd, because he thought that, in this at any rate, a heart of stone was what he had – and he had been wrong.

Still, there was the question of justice. He went into the hedgerow, cut the reddest rose he could find, and saddled his horse. He had a good idea where his victim might be.

After Blakiston had gone, and Kate had completed her chores, she set off to walk to the mean cottage in which Rosie Miller had grown up. Before she had moved with Tom and Lizzie to Chopwell Garth, it would have been a journey of less than five minutes; now it took longer, but Kate was every bit as light in spirits as Blakiston had been after their conversation and, in any case, she was used to walking. What was going to be more difficult was becoming accustomed to travelling on horseback or in a carriage, and she knew that those things were going to be required of her after her marriage, at least from time to time.

Rosie's mother received her with delight, harassed though she was by looking after Rosie's boisterous younger sisters and brothers. Kate seized the youngest in her arms. 'Be still. Sit with me, and I will tell you a story.' The child stared solemnly into her eyes, silenced by this unknown face, and the others gathered round. 'Us too! Tell the story to all of us!'

And so Kate told them the story of Noah and the flood. And then she told them the story of Adam and Eve. And then she told them the story of Joseph and his brothers. By the time she was finished the third story, Rosie's mother was sitting exhausted on the settle but the spell of peace from the babble of children all demanding attention had allowed her to finish her housekeeping jobs much faster than she would normally have been able to do. She smiled at Kate – a smile full of weariness but a smile, too, that conveyed her pleasure in seeing Rosie's old friend again. 'Kate! I heard your wonderful news in church. Is all well?'

'It is. The banns will be told for the third time on Sunday and the week after that we will be free to wed. I wondered… Does Rosie know that I am to marry?'

'She does. And she is as pleased for you as I am.'

'Mr Blakiston…' Kate paused, embarrassed, looking for the words. 'He insists… I have told him it is not necessary but he says it must be…'

And now Rosie's mother's face was wreathed in smiles and she said, 'He says you must have a maid. And you would like Rosie.'

'Do you think she will be angry with me for even thinking about asking her?'

'Oh, Kate. She will be as happy as I am. And I could not be happier. She will be safe. Safe from those dreadful Blackett men.'

'You don't think it might be…'

'Awkward? Of course, it could be. But that would be up to the two of you. And you have known each other since you were children, and you have always been friends, so there is no need for any awkwardness at all, unless you choose to let it happen. You want me to get word to her – that is why you have come?'

'It is. I don't want – that is, Mr Blakiston does not want…'

'To go anywhere near Matfen Hall. I understand. Everyone has heard about the offer the Blacketts made him.'

'He will not be happy when I tell him that.'

'Well, it is true. And it is to his credit. Though not so much to his credit as the fact that he asked you to be his wife, instead.' She turned to the eldest of the children who still sat on the ground around Kate's feet. 'Tommy. I want you to run to Matfen Hall. Go to the kitchen door and ask for your sister. Don't say anything about the conversation you have just overheard. Tell our Rosie that I need to speak to her as soon as she can get away. Have you got that?'

Tommy nodded, and a girl of about ten years of age said, 'Can I go with him, our mam?'

'Yes, Martha, you can go with him. Make sure the pair of you go straight there and then come straight back. Wait.' She went into the cott, and when she came back she was carrying bread and cheese. 'Matfen Hall is the other side of the Tyne. You will be gone for hours. Take this with you, but don't eat it until you have seen Rosie and given her the message.'

Kate stood up. 'Thank you. It would be wonderful if Rosie said yes, but I hope she won't hate me for asking.'

'Don't you worry about that, girl. She will be as glad as I am.' She smiled. 'I'd better not call you girl again, had I? Not with you moving into the gentry.' And they both laughed.

Chapter 18

Wilkin Longstaff was at least fifty years old and farmed two hundred acres of land belonging to the Bishop of Durham with the help of two of his sons. When they came in for dinner that evening, Wilkin's wife Sarah had a story to tell them. Their granddaughter Matilda believed that a man had been watching her. Watching her in a way that she did not like. 'She said it frightened her,' said Sarah.

'She's eight years old,' said Longstaff. 'It's the sort of story that children of that age tell.'

Sarah said, 'She's a very sensible girl. Her head is screwed on. She doesn't go around making things up.'

'Did she recognise him? I haven't heard of any strangers in the area.'

'She said he was wearing a big hat and cloak and his face was covered.'

'Come on, woman. This is a child's make-believe.'

'She said he was carrying a rose. Would a child make up a story like that?'

'Well,' said Longstaff, 'tell her to keep her eye out and, if she sees him again, to run here and tell me or her father.' And he put it out of his mind. But the maid had heard the conversation and, two days later, she told a friend of hers who was a maid in another farmhouse. And two days after that, the friend told another friend who worked in yet a third farmhouse about the man of threatening appearance who had so frightened young Matilda.

And then it was Sunday, and the banns were told for the third time, and no-one made any objection, and now any doubt that Kate may have entertained about what the future held disappeared. She and Blakiston were free to marry. Unless something happened to one or other of them, they would do so the following Sunday.

Florrie had taken on the task of sewing the dress that Kate would wear. She hadn't been asked – she had volunteered. It was something she wanted to do, and it gave her the opportunity to fuss around the bride to be, making sure that she would look the best she possibly could.

This was a new departure for the Greener family. When they had married in the past, they had done so in their ordinary day-to-day clothes – their rags for the most part – because that was what they had, and there had been no money for fripperies. The reality was that, in the case of most of those marriages, the bride had already been pregnant at the time the marriage took place because that was the custom. A very necessary custom. When a working man grew too old to work, he knew that if he relied on the overseers of the poor, his life would be a poor and straitened thing. Women knew the same. If their final years were to be anything other than miserable, men and women knew that they must marry only someone who had shown a particular and very important ability.

Men must show that they could father a child so that they could be looked after when they were too old to look after themselves. And women must show that they could conceive and bear such a child.

It was not that way for Kate and Blakiston. Kate knew that, if it was her fate to be widowed, Blakiston would leave her with a sufficient competence to keep herself and any children she may have borne. And Blakiston knew that, should he suffer the fate of being widowed himself, he would be able to support himself and hire someone to cook, clean and look after their children.

For all that, the dress Florrie was making had nothing of the frivolous about it. It was a dress in which Kate would look a fitting bride for her husband, but it was also a dress that she could wear in her daily life without feeling out of place or oddly arrayed.

That evening, Blakiston dined at the rector's house for the last time as a single man. Lady Isabella said to him over dinner, 'Mister Blakiston. I have talked about this to Thomas and we are of one mind. What arrangements have you made for a meal to celebrate your marriage?'

'It shames me to say, Lady Isabella, that I have as yet made none. I have been too busy. You know, the harvest is not yet completed. But I had thought to invite you and Thomas and my brother – and, of course, Kate's family – to dine with me at the inn.'

'That is what we thought. And what we also thought was that it would be an honour for us if you allowed us to make the arrangements for you. You know we have the barn where, not long from now, we will hold the harvest supper. We would like to invite you and Kate, her family, and everyone who is in the church when the wedding takes place, to join us there afterwards for a meal. We have spoken to Walter Wilson, the butcher, and he can not only provide us with an entire pig and some chickens but will also roast and carve them. Rosina will see to the puddings and the vegetables, and Thomas will I am sure be prevailed on to provide enough wine for the gathering, at least so long as I ensure a sufficiency of cheese.'

Blakiston was almost overwhelmed by the kindness of the offer. 'Lady Isabella, I hesitate to impose on you to such an extent…'

'Hesitate all you like, but accept. We are agreed.' And she signalled that the serving of the evening's meal should begin.

While they were eating, Isabella said, 'I have been thinking about the grave on which the Hindmarsh boy's body was left. You know it was a pauper's grave and I have wondered what that has to tell us.'

'You think we should be looking for a pauper?'

'I think we should be thinking about overseers. Overseers of the poor, that is, not overseers like you. For young Ezra Hindmarsh may have been left on a pauper's grave, but he was no pauper. His grandfather, though, was an overseer. And Margaret, who was married to Joseph Laws – her father was an overseer.'

'Surely, my dear,' said her husband, the rector, 'that is merely coincidence?'

'Well, perhaps. But it is at least something that might bear thinking about.'

Blakiston nodded. She might well be right – though where it took them, and how he might use the information, he could not imagine. And so the conversation passed to other things, and the meal was completed in leisurely fashion and with great pleasure for all three, after which Lady Isabella left the two men to their cheese and brandy, and the rector to his pipe of tobacco.

Blakiston might well have done nothing with the thought passed on by the rector's wife, had it not been for a piece of information that came his way two days later. He had called at Chopwell Garth, to ensure that the harvested corn was being well looked after but also because he hated a day to pass without contact with the woman he was soon to marry.

Kate said, 'I heard something this morning that may interest you concerning the deaths of Margaret Laws and Ezra Hindmarsh.'

'And what was that?'

'There is a farmer called Wilkin Longstaff. You may not know him, for he farms the Bishop's land. But he has a maid who passed on a story to a friend who is a maid to another farmer. And she passed it on to another friend...'

'And another maid at another farm?'

'That is so, James. And, you know, farmers maids have friends who are maids at other farms...'

'And so the story was passed on yet again?'

'It was. And this time, the maid who received the story works here, at Chopwell Garth.'

'And so you have heard the story?'

'I have. It seems that Wilkin Longstaff has two sons, and one of them has a daughter called Matilda. And Matilda was disturbed by the way a man was looking at her. Watching her.'

'Did she recognise this man?'

'She did not. He wore a hat pulled down on his head, his face was largely covered and he wore a wide flowing cloak.'

'That is a pity. But I do not see…'

'James. The man she saw carried a red rose.'

'Ah. Now, that *is* interesting. Because a red rose was found beside the body of Ezra Hindmarsh, and I have assumed that the killer left it there.'

'And such a rose was also left at Hope House Farm when Joseph's wife Margaret was killed.'

'You are right. Of course, there is no reason why someone should not be carrying a rose and we cannot assume for certain that whoever looked at Matilda Longstaff was the killer I have been seeking. Nevertheless…'

'It is an interesting coincidence.'

'It is indeed.'

'Will you have Joseph released from Durham jail?'

'It is not as simple as that, Kate. I have no such authority. The only person who can be relied on to release him is the only person who could also hang him – the Assize Court Judge. And I should still like to have his explanation as to why he attacked me. But I think I may speak to the rector, who is a Justice of the Peace, and ask his advice.'

'And Matilda Longstaff? What will you do about her?'

'I think I shall speak to Wilkin Longstaff and tell him to exercise great care.'

But, later, Blakiston decided that that was not enough. Lady Isabella's remarks about paupers and overseers had combined with Kate's news about Matilda Longstaff and an unknown watcher to suggest something else he could also do. And so, after calling in at the Longstaff's farm and telling Wilkin Longstaff to take care of his granddaughter, Blakiston rode onwards to see Walter Maughan.

Chapter 19

He was met at the Maughan farm with the same civility as previously. He was shown into the parlour and served with coffee, fruit cake and cheese, just as before. Tasting the sharp cheese, he wondered whether the rector had ever been a guest in this house. If Maughan was correct, then the rector disapproved of Maughan's possession of a pew and of the way his servants shared it. The rector might regard the farmer as being too far beneath him socially for this sort of intercourse. If so, that would be a shame, because the rector with his love of cheese and plain speaking would have enjoyed the hospitality of the house. But the enjoyment of hospitality was not the purpose of this visit.

'Maughan,' said Blakiston. 'I have a question to ask you.'

The farmer's eyebrows raised in a mute signal that Blakiston should proceed.

'Your daughter died at the hands of some villain as yet unidentified. And so did the grandchild of Ezra Hindmarsh.'

'That is true.'

'The question I would like to ask is this. Did you ever sit as an overseer of the poor with Ezra

Hindmarsh and Wilkin Longstaff to examine the case of a pauper?'

A look of shock passed across Maughan's face. 'Longstaff? Oh no! Surely he has not also been visited by this murderous person?'

'He has not lost anyone. Or not yet. But there is reason to think that his granddaughter Matilda may have been watched by the person we seek.'

'Longstaff is a good man. I doubt not that his granddaughter is a good girl. He must be warned.'

'I have already taken care of that, Maughan. But my question?'

'The answer to your question, Blakiston, is: yes. Hindmarsh, Longstaff and me, we have sat together. And more than once.'

'That is what I was afraid you would say.' And yet, he thought, it is also what I hoped you would say, because perhaps it may be the first step on the path that will lead us to a solution to this awful mystery. 'So now I must ask you to rack your brains and search your memory and give me the name of every pauper whose case the three of you have supervised together.'

'Mister Blakiston. I first sat with both of those gentlemen a goodly number of years ago. And we have done it since, too, because, you know, an overseer of the poor serves for a period and is then excused while someone else takes his place, but is then elected to serve again. We three may have sat together three or four times over a long period. And that would take in a great many paupers.'

'I don't ask for an immediate answer, Maughan, although I would like to receive a list as soon as possible. It may be that I will find on that list the name of the person I seek.'

'I will do it, of course. But it will mean consulting the minutes books of the overseers of the poor in all three chapelries over a long period, first to find those times when we three sat together and then to find the names of the paupers we discussed. It may be a week or so before I can give you an answer.'

'Then a week or so it will have to be. I suppose there is no name so glaring that it occurs to you immediately?'

He could see that Maughan was thinking hard, but then the farmer shook his head. 'I'm sorry. There is nothing that springs immediately to mind.'

'No matter. When you have an answer, send word and I shall come to examine your list. Will you be in church this Sunday?'

'I am in church every Sunday, Mister Blakiston.'

'Then you will witness my marriage to Kate Greener.'

'And a great deal of pleasure it will give me, sir.'

'Thank you for that, but the reason I ask is to say that the rector intends to invite all those who are present in the church at the time of my marriage to join us all in the rectory's barn for a meal in celebration.'

'And our servants? Are they to be invited, too?'

'I did say *all* who are present.'

'Then we will be delighted to accept the rector's invitation. Sir, I look forward to celebrating in your company.' He smiled. 'I look forward also to seeing how Susannah Bent responds to the rector's invitation,'

Next morning, Tom and Ned armed themselves with stout cudgels for defence against footpads and set off in the cart to visit Joseph Laws in Durham jail. They carried with them two sets of clean clothes and a basket of victuals put up by Lizzie.

When they reached the jail, Ned was so incensed by the hostile welcome from the jailer that Tom had to put a restraining hand on his arm. He gave the jailer three pennies, as Blakiston had recommended, and asked him to bring a bowl of water so that Joseph could wash before putting on a change of clothes.

'Joseph,' said Tom. 'Mister Blakiston knows by now that you probably did not kill your wife.'

'Probably? *Probably*! Do you doubt it?'

'Joseph, I have been sure from the beginning that it was someone else who strangled Margaret to death. And now young Ezra Hindmarsh has been done away with in the same way, and that could not have been you because you were here. And since that happened, it seems very likely that the person who killed Margaret and the Hindmarsh boy was on the verge of killing Matilda Longstaff – and you were still in here.'

'There you are, then. If the second and third were not me, who could believe that I was responsible for the first? And if that is so, then why have I not been released?' He had by this time finished his ablutions and was gratefully casting aside the clothes he had been wearing and donning new. He pointed at the ones he had dropped to the floor. 'Those will be fit now only for burning.'

'Perhaps,' said Tom. 'But we will take them home and let Florrie and Lizzie make the final judgement. Joseph, you have not been released because no-one can understand why, if you had done nothing, you attacked Mister Blakiston in the way you did. Give me something I can take back to him. An explanation.'

Joseph took from the basket a hunk of bread and a slice of ham. He stared at the floor. 'I never wanted to marry Margaret. In fact, I disliked her. When we were alone in private, she had nothing good to say about anyone but herself. You, Ned here, Lizzie – and as for what she said about Kate... Well, you don't want to hear it and that is as well because I'm not going to say it.'

'We know all that, Joseph. You took Margaret as a wife so that you would not lose your farm. Everyone knows that, including Mister Blakiston. You are not the first person to have accepted marriage with someone they did not want in order to gain something they did. Look at Lizzie and me – she made it clear from the very beginning that she wanted nothing to do with me and it took a very long time before we came together as man and wife.'

'That would never have happened with Margaret and me. And you wanted Lizzie, long before you knew she was carrying Wrekin's bairn. So, in the end, you got what you wanted. And I did not, because the person I wanted was Kate.'

'Kate!'

'The moment you moved into Chopwell Garth and Lizzie brought her family with her – Ned here, Florrie and Kate – I looked at Kate and I knew from that first moment that she was someone I could be happy with. I had already begun to feel that, just from seeing them in church, but seeing her close like that – hearing her talk, understanding what a good person she was, listening to that clear, firm voice – I wanted her.'

'Did you ever tell her that?'

'I did. I was mebbes clumsy, because it was so important to me and I have not the way of speaking to women. And she was nice about it, and she did not make me feel bad, but she told me it could never be. And I knew she meant it. And so, when I knew I must have a wife or lose the farm and end up a collier, I looked around for someone else. And there was no-one but Margaret. She put herself forward, you know.'

'Did she, the hussy?'

'Well, she did. She came to see me and she said she knew I must be wanting a wife, and she was wanting a husband. She said she knew what people said about her and she said she had not always been the person she should have been, but she was older now and she knew what was needed of her. She said she would be a good wife to me, and faithful. And she was Walter Maughan's daughter – a farmer's daughter – so she knew the life. And so I accepted her.' He had finished the ham and now took a slice of beef. 'This is so good, compared with what we get to eat here. And we only get that if we can pay the jailer.'

'Mister Blakiston has sent you some money. I have it here. Lord Ravenshead has told him he can spend what he needs to keep you fed and clothed.'

'That is good of his Lordship.'

'It is good also of Mister Blakiston,' said Tom.

'Yes, yes, it is good also of Mister Blakiston, but you cannot expect me to feel grateful to the man who will wed the woman I loved and who is the one who keeps me in here.'

'He is also the man who might get you out. If I am able to take back proper answers to the questions I have asked you. And a proper answer would not be that you had wanted to marry the young woman that Mister Blakiston is engaged to.'

'Well, I did. But I had given up on that. I have told you so. And I had married someone else. But when I saw him – Blakiston, the overseer – and I saw Kate, and I saw how they looked at each other, and I compared that exchange of feelings with the way I felt about Margaret – it was a stupid thing to do. I knew that when I did it.'

'You were jealous? was that the sum of it?'

'It was. For Margaret led me such a dance. She had said she would be a good wife to me, and faithful, and she was not. That first night we lay together – the night we were wed – she laughed at me.'

Tom looked at his brother. Not for the first time, he thanked God for the fate that had matched him to Lizzie and not to someone like Margaret. Tom's face resembled the darkness of clouds before a storm and Tom wondered just how close to madness Joseph might have been brought. He said, 'She was not faithful to you?'

Joseph shook his head. 'After that first night... We never again...'

'Mister Blakiston said that she bore the bruises of a number of beatings.'

'The law gives a man the right to mate with his wife. And I tried to take by force what she refused to give me by right. Did you never do the same with Lizzie?'

Tom shook his head. He was more shocked than he wanted to admit to himself. 'Never. There was a long time after we married when she refused me her bed.'

'And you never forced the issue?' Joseph looked as though he found this difficult to believe.

'Never. In fact, it was not until Ned here, her brother, had been taken by the press men and I was shot and close to death getting him out of their clutches that she found that she loved me after all... That she had come to love me... And since then... She has been my wife and I have been her husband. This child Margaret carried...?'

'It could not possibly have been mine. But I did not kill her for it, Tom. You must believe that.'

'I do. And I will tell Mister Blakiston that. And we will see what he chooses to do about it. But here. Take this money. And give me back that basket. Ned, do you pick up those filthy clothes and we will see what Florrie and Lizzie can do with them. Joseph, we will be back soon. Do not allow your spirits to sink as low as they did when you attacked Mister Blakiston.'

Ned said, 'The letter, Tom. You have forgot the letter.'

'So I have. Joseph, you said that Margaret read to you a letter from some Lord telling you to meet him in a pub that was as imaginary as the lord was. Mister Blakiston asked you to show him the letter, but you could not.'

'It did exist. I was not lying.'

'We know it existed, because the post boy said he delivered it. And it had been paid for. But there was no sign of any letter in Hope House Farm when Jeffrey Drabble and Mister Blakiston searched for it. So where did it come from? Who sent it? Why did they do so? And where is it now?'

'I do not know. When I realised I had been made a fool of and sent all that way for no reason, I thought Margaret had done it so that she would have a night with some man and me out of the house. I can tell you I was in such a fury by the time I got home. And then, of course, I found her lying dead and I did what I could not imagine doing which was to leave Samuel alone in the house with his dead mother while I rode to Chopwell Garth. That was a measure of the confusion I was in.'

'What did you think when you found her lying there?'

'That God's justice had been done. That she had betrayed me with another, and the one she betrayed me with had killed her.'

'We will tell all of this to Mister Blakiston. And we will be back soon as we can to bring whatever news there is.'

Chapter 20

He hadn't been able to do it. He had wanted to do it; he was aware of his duty to do it – a duty owed to those who had themselves been condemned to death and on whose behalf he had condemned this girl – but, in the end, he had not been able to do it. It wasn't fear of being caught; he would prefer not to hang, but if that turned out to be the price he had to pay for four deaths administered in justice, he would pay it. It wasn't that he lacked the strength or the opportunity; his ability to overpower such a victim was unquestioned and the opportunity had been there, staring him in the face. But he hadn't been able to do it.

He told himself that this was merely a delay, a short interruption to his plans, and that he would execute the girl within the next few days and deal with his fourth and final victim after that. And he did not believe it.

He was reduced almost to tears by the way old Ezra Hindmarsh grieved for his lost grandson. Was he to inflict the same grief on Wilkin Longstaff? Longstaff deserved it – that was not in question – and Hindmarsh had deserved it, too. But pain is pain and inflicting it hurt more than he would ever have believed. He had grieved for those he had lost and he had believed that inflicting that same pain on those responsible for his losses was not only justifiable but also right.

Perhaps, if he had stayed away, got someone else to carry out the work, and heard about it at a distance, all would have been well. But that was not how it had been. He had killed these people himself. And he had seen Hindmarsh afterwards.

The killing of Margaret Laws had been a false start. It had caused him no pain at all, the woman herself had been a detestable trollop, Walter Maughan had given no sign of being troubled and any grief caused to Joseph Laws was the result only of losing his farm and being cast into jail for attacking the overseer. When he had finished with Margaret Laws, he was reinforced in the view that he was doing the right thing. An eye for an eye. A life for a life. One life for one life and three more lives to be claimed for three that had been taken. The way of justice.

But the Hindmarsh boy had been different. Just like those four he could never forget, the Hindmarsh boy had had his whole life in front of him. And he had taken it away. He did not believe in God, but he certainly knew that God was not him – and yet, he had acted like a god.

And then he had gone to the place where he knew he would find Longstaff's granddaughter. His heart had been full of thoughts of vengeance;

that now Longstaff would know the pain of loss that Longstaff had once caused him to know himself. Justice would be done. You took mine; I take yours. And he had not been able to do it.

Was he really going to be able to return? Would he, next time, carry out the act of vengeance that he had not been able to commit this time? He told himself that he would. He knew, deep in his heart, that he was wrong.

What now? He had not the faintest idea. But he had done himself the most serious damage. There had to be a way to put things right.

Thomas Claverley was not a foolish man and neither was he an unworldly one. He knew that not all of his parishioners were firm believers in the God that Thomas as rector of Ryton parish preached every Sunday in the Church of the Holy Cross. That was all right; this was not the time of Oliver Cromwell and the puritans; it was enough that people came to the House of God without demanding control over what they believed. Some came from a fervent dedication to the Lord. Kate Greener was one of those, and Kate would soon be married to James Blakiston, who most certainly was not. If this caused any difficulty between husband and wife, it was a matter for them alone. Thomas would not intervene. James Blakiston came to church because his employer, Lord Ravenshead, expected him to. Others came for the social occasion – to see neighbours who they might not meet again for a whole week, to exchange news and simply to gossip. Some – and here the rector thought with a sad smile of the disappointed Susannah Bent – came in the hope of attracting the attention of a suitor.

Thomas had once been astonished to find Blakiston on his knees in the church. It had been when the overseer was looking for the murderer of old Reuben Cooper, but Blakiston's presence in church had been nothing to do with that. Blakiston had been grieving over the ill-treatment he had once meted out to a trusting young woman in his home parish in Hampshire and it had been clear to the rector that what had fired this regret had been the overseer's newly discovered love for a woman Blakiston refused to name that day – the woman he was finally to wed this coming Sunday.

Thomas felt a similar astonishment now, because he was under no illusions about Job King: King did not believe a word of the Gospels and the sermons he heard in this place each Sunday, and yet here he was on his knees just as Blakiston had once been. Something must be going on in the man's head to have brought this about.

Thomas knelt beside him. 'Job King. It is good to see you here. Is there anything you would like to discuss with me?'

King shook his head. 'Nothing, Rector. The lease is coming to an end and I must soon decide between staying here permanently and returning to the colonies.'

'You seek God's guidance on the matter?'

A hint of a smile touched the corners of King's lips. 'You know, it is a big decision, and would involve a long and sometimes hazardous journey. I must seek inspiration from every possible source.'

The rector smiled. He knew that he had not received an answer to his question but, as he had expected none, he was untroubled. 'Well, Mister King, we have grown used to seeing you here and the parish is better for your presence. And especially the parish's poorer members. Whatever decision you arrive at, I wish God's blessing upon you.'

Chapter 21

While the rector was talking to Job King, Blakiston was speaking to Tom Laws, who wanted to unburden himself of the conversation with his brother at Durham jail. Blakiston said, 'So that was the only reason he attempted to brain me? Because he had formed a desire for Kate and thought that I would stand in his way? Rightly, of course, for I would and do.'

'That is what he says, Master.'

'And you believe him?'

'Yes, Master. I do.'

'Hmm. Well, I suppose it may be so. It was foolish, for he had no hope of ever winning Kate for himself and he caused himself to be thrown into that dreadful place.'

'Do you think he could now be released, Master?'

'I don't know, Tom. I have no power to release him. The rector is a Justice of the Peace; I shall ask his advice.'

'Thank you, Master. Master, Joseph's time in there has already been…'

'Yes, Tom, I know what you want to say. I will get the rector's advice as quickly as I can. In fact, although I have other things to do, I shall go there now. If the rector says the word, Joseph can be released today.'

'Thank you, Master.'

And so Blakiston put aside what he had intended to do next in order to consult the rector about the release of Joseph Laws. Before he could get to the point of his visit, he had to listen to Thomas's report of Job King's visit. 'He said he was seeking guidance on whether he should remain here when his lease falls due or whether he should return to the Americas.'

'Thomas, you speak those words with a certain touch of doubt.'

'Oh, James, you of all people know that unaccustomed visitors do not always tell the whole truth to the vicar when they are found in church and on their knees, for you did not.'

'That is true, Thomas. And so, what do you think might have been the reason for his prayers?'

'I have no idea. And it may have been as he said. But he seemed in pain. You know, it is sometimes only when they find themselves *in extremis* that people who have not previously shown an inclination to ardent worship turn to the church. Something may have troubled Job King as the man from whom he takes his name was troubled. Who can tell? If he finds himself in such need of solace that he turns to me, then I shall know – but, of course, I will not be able to tell you. It will be a matter between him, me and God. But since his explanation was such a clear falsehood, I need not be troubled to keep his confidence. Now. Tell me what brings you here?'

And Blakiston did, and Thomas said that the prisoner could be released on his written say-so, but that he recommended that no release take place until the following Monday.

'Why the delay?' asked Blakiston.

'Because you are to be married on Sunday and it was an ill-conceived passion for your bride that caused Laws to launch his attack on you. Do you not feel that it would be better to keep him away from here on Sunday?'

Blakiston gave that a little thought and then agreed.

'And where is he to go after his release?' said Thomas. 'Back to Hope House Farm?'

'No,' said Blakiston, amazed at himself that he had so far failed to address that simple question. 'He has no wife; his farm will either become part of Chopwell Garth or another farmer will take over its running; I doubt that he would wish to be a labourer on his younger brother's farm; I doubt equally that his younger brother would think that a good idea; and in any case we have enough labourers. He will have to go to one of the mining villages that are springing up, may God help him.'

'He has no wife,' agreed Thomas, 'but he does have a small child. He cannot look after the boy while he is underground. And he certainly cannot take the boy there with him.'

Blakiston reflected on the rector's words. Joseph Laws had damaged Blakiston's knee and attempted to beat his brains from his skull. Blakiston could not have been criticised if he had decided that the man must simply take his chances in the world. But it was not as simple as that. Joseph Laws was the brother of Tom Laws and Tom Laws was married to Kate's older sister, Lizzie. He said, 'You raise important questions, Thomas. I shall have to think on them.'

'I suggest you do so before he is released from prison and not afterwards.'

Chapter 22

As it happened, a similar conversation was taking place at Chopwell Garth. When Tom and Ned had returned with the news that Mister Blakiston would ask the rector how to get Joseph Laws released from prison, Florrie said that they had better know before Joseph came out what they were going to do about him. The last time Joseph's future had been discussed – before he had assaulted Blakiston – Kate had had wished upon her a removal to Hope House Farm that she had very much resented. She was grateful now that she would be married and away from the farm and so would not be involved in whatever was decided. In fact, she did not even need to take part in the discussion – and so she did not.

Lizzie said, 'Tom, you don't want him to live here, do you?'

'I don't see how he can, even if I did want it. He can't be a labourer here. I could not afford to pay him anything but a labourer's wages, I would have to lay someone else off and I don't believe that Mister Blakiston would let me.'

Florrie said, 'No. But there is the question of little Samuel.'

With a severity that surprised the others, Lizzie said, 'Samuel is not Joseph's child.'

'No,' said Florrie, 'but that is not Samuel's fault and the law and the church – and the overseers of the poor – would say that Joseph is Samuel's father.'

Tom said, 'Joseph can't keep Samuel with him unless he has a wife to look after the boy.'

'Not unless they lived here,' said Florrie.

'Which we have already agreed Joseph is not going to do,' said Lizzie. 'Oh, I know you think I'm being hard, and mebbes I am, but I'm trying to avoid trouble and trouble there would be eventually if Joseph lived here where Tom – his younger brother – is the farmer and Joseph is picking up whatever work there may be. Samuel can live here, of course he can, for as long as he needs to and until he is grown up if that's how it happens. We already have Lulu; what is one more child to care for? If Joseph gets himself a wife and wants Samuel with him, then of course Samuel will have to go.'

Florrie said, 'That would be a terrible wrench for the boy if it doesn't happen for a year or two. He'd be settled here with us and then have to go somewhere else where he didn't know them. Because, by that time, he will not know Joseph.'

'Yes,' said Tom, 'and it's a pity, but he'd hardly be unusual. You raised Lizzie and Kate and Ned, but you weren't the mother to all three because

Lizzie's mam died and her father married you because he needed a mother for her and her older brother.' No-one raised an eyebrow at this because it was a simple statement of fact. Life among the labouring classes in 1760s Durham was precarious. If a man or a woman died with children still at home and not of working age, the one who was left married again – and, almost always, more children were born. If there was another adult death, the family would go through the whole cycle again. These were not love matches; they were born of necessity but for the most part they worked. People made them work. It was better to be in a marriage where there was at least some degree of affection than one totally without love.

Florrie said, 'No, it would not be unusual, but it would still be a wrench. In any case, if Joseph is not to work on this farm, and if we can assume that Mister Blakiston would be unhappy to have him working on another…'

'And I think we can assume that,' said Tom.

'Then what is to become of him?'

'He must go either to a pit village where he can work in the mines or to a town where he can work in a manufactory,' said Lizzie. 'I'm sorry, Tom, I know he's your brother and I know no-one who has spent his whole life working on the land is going to want to work beneath it, but the facts are the facts.'

Tom nodded. 'I know that. I think Joseph will know it, too. He has been a fool. A fool to marry a woman like Margaret and an even bigger fool to attack Mister Blakiston.'

Lizzie said, 'Do we need to discuss this – do *you* need to discuss this – with Mister Blakiston?'

'I don't know whether I need to or not, but I know that not a day passes without him arriving here apparently to talk to me about work but really to bill and coo with your sister there. He's bound to turn up today and I shall tell him then what we have decided.'

Kate laughed.

Later that day, it was Blakiston's turn to laugh, and this time with delight when he was on his way to Hope House Farm to make sure, now that the harvest was over, that everything there was as it should be in the absence of a permanent farmer. He heard the rapid drumming of hooves behind that said someone was in a hurry to catch up with him. He reined in Obsidian and turned, one hand on the butt of a pistol – but this was no highwayman. It was his brother, Peter, a naval officer now on shore leave and here to be his groom's man. The two leapt from their horses, swept the three-cornered hats from their heads and clasped each other's shoulders – the closest English men of their class and generation could possibly come to embracing each other.

'Peter! My dear chap! But how did you know where to find me?'

'I arrived at the inn not thirty minutes ago. They are looking after my horse; they gave me the use of this one. And they told me the road you had been seen riding down and the place they believed you might be going to. And here you are.'

'And here I am.' Blakiston raised himself once more into the saddle. 'And delighted to see you. Ride with me. There is a farm I wish to visit and after that we shall return to the inn, take some breakfast, and you must give me all your news.'

As they rode along, Blakiston said, 'Did you come straight here from the port?'

'I have been two days in Burley.' As he said this, his manner lost a little of its brightness.

'Ah. And have you news of Burley doings?'

'Much, brother. But I think there are only two people there who would concern you now.' Blakiston waited in silence. Peter went on, 'She to whom you were once engaged married another.'

'Yes. I knew that.'

'But I think you did not know that she died in giving birth to her first child.'

Blakiston fell silent. Both men knew the dreadful risks that women took when they became pregnant. Every time a woman gave birth, she faced a possibility of more than one in a hundred that she would not survive more than ten days after the birth. Peter let him absorb the news without interruption and then said, 'The child did not survive.'

'I am sorry.'

'Yes.' What else was there to say?

'And the other?'

Peter's face brightened. 'I believe the overseers of the poor no longer claim against your bastardy bond.'

'That is true. Not this year, and not last. Is the child dead?'

'No, for I have seen him and he looks in fine fettle. His mother married a schoolmaster. From what I've seen, I believe she is happy. And she has given her new husband a daughter to go with the son you left for him.'

'I am glad. I was thoughtless and callous towards her. I thank the fates that have brought her to this better life.' They both knew, as they knew the dangers faced by pregnant women, how difficult it could be for a respectable young woman to overcome the shame of a child born out of wedlock enough to find a husband. 'Her schoolmaster must be a good man. Now, this is Hope House Farm and I must talk to the people here. Come with me.'

It was clear that Susannah the maid was pleased to see Blakiston. 'Master. Jemmy Rayne wishes to fix a date for our wedding. William Snowball left here after the harvest, and Dick Jackson comes here now only to sleep and eat.'

'Does he indeed? The impertinence.'

'Well, Master, I am pleased that he does since no-one is coming for the eggs and I need to find a use for them. Jeffrey Drabble is still here, of course. But, sir, I need to give an answer to Jemmy Rayne, or he may believe I do not want to wed him and he may look for someone else.'

Blakiston smiled. They could not allow that to happen – when all was said and done, a maid with a temper like Susannah's would struggle to find another good man and Blakiston knew that a good man was what Rayne was. He said, 'Where is Drabble now?'

'I am here, sir,' said Drabble. 'When you arrived, I was...' He gestured through the back door to where the privy was sited on the other side of the yard.

Blakiston felt rather than saw his brother's smothered smile. 'Well, these things must be taken care of. And you are still here as caretaker.'

'Yes, sir. Sir, we heard that Joseph Laws might be released soon. Will he return here as farmer?'

'He will not. I have a decision to make and the decision is: do I find a new farmer for Hope House or do I join it with Chopwell Garth? I will make that decision this week. As soon as I make it, you will be released, Drabble.' He turned to Susannah. 'You, too. Whoever takes over here will need to bring a maid of their own. You may tell Jemmy Rayne that you will be at his command from Sunday on.'

'Thank you, Master. And Dick Jackson? Am I to continue to give him his breakfast?'

'Until Drabble leaves here and ceases to want his company, you may do so. After that, not. And I shall see that someone is taking care of the eggs from next week. What of butter and cheese? You are still milking the cows, I take it?'

'Master, because no-one was taking it away, I have made only enough butter for me and the two men. The rest of the milk has gone into making more cheese, because cheese does not suffer from being left on the shelf in the way that butter does.'

Indeed,' said Blakiston, 'in fact it improves. Drabble, take some of the older cheese and carry it to the rector. Tell him it comes from me. The rector can never have too much cheese.' He turned to his brother. 'Let us return now to the inn.'

When they got there, Blakiston said, 'This inn is comfortable, as inns go, but would you not rather stay in my house?"

Peter smiled. 'Brother, when I am next hereabouts I shall accept your offer with thanks. But on Sunday, you are to be married, and on Sunday night you and your bride will have no need – and no wish, I make no doubt – for strangers in your house. You will wish to be alone. And I shall respect that wish by remaining here.'

The same thought had occurred to Blakiston, and he made no objection.

'You have to find a farmer for that place we just visited. I am a seafaring man and I understand nothing of how these things are done. What will you do?'

'In fact, a plan is forming. I intend to ask Tom Laws at Chopwell Garth farm to take charge of Hope House as well. But he will need help. And there is a man who has experience of labouring at Hope House and who, I believe, is ready for more responsibility. His alternative is to work underground in the coal mines, a fate dreaded by farmworkers but one that too many of them have had to accept. He has no wife, which is normally a requirement in a farmer as far as I am concerned, but he has a mother. And he has a younger brother. I shall see Tom Laws later today, and I shall ask him to speak to Emmett Batey and see whether they can work together.'

Peter nodded. 'You know, the normal way to a commission in the Navy is to buy it. As our kinsman bought mine for me. But, in the heat of battle, officers as well as men are killed and it is not unusual to promote an ordinary seaman. Some of them have the brains and the common sense to perform as well as an educated man, even though they have been recruited from the lowest ranks of society. So even do better.'

'And that is what I find here. The Tom Laws I mentioned is one of the best farmers in the county, and yet if it had not been for the purest chance he would now be either a common labourer of the lowest type and the meanest income or he, too, would have had to go to the mines. It is a tragedy for this country that we waste so many good people for no reason other than an accident of birth. If we can raise enough people like Tom Laws and Emmett Batey, and if people see us doing it and observe the results, we may change minds. But I doubt it. And now, Brother, I invite you to take some rest while I go to Chopwell Garth to talk to Tom Laws.'

'Chopwell Garth? And I think that Tom Laws is not the only person you go there to speak to.'

'It is true: my beloved is there, too.'

'Then you must take me with you, for it cannot be too soon for me to meet the woman our sister says has bewitched you. But you said something of breakfast?'

'I have eaten. But I shall sit here while you have yours, and you may tell me what Hannah had to say to you. And how you responded.'

That evening, when Dick Jackson came to Hope House Farm, he had news to discuss with Jeffrey Drabble. 'Did Job King ever ask you to work for him? I suggested he should.'

'I heard he was looking for me. But I was so busy with Mister Blakiston's new-fangled ways with the harvest, and Margaret Laws's murder, and having to chase after Joseph Laws, that we never met.'

'That could be a pity. Because today he made an offer to all his workers and, if you'd been one of them, I might have accepted.'

'Offer? What was this offer?'

'To go back to the colonies with him.'

'He does not mean to stay here, then,' said Drabble.

'It seems not. And, from what he told us about life in the American colonies, I do not blame him.'

Susannah Ward had been listening at the door. Now she stepped forward. 'I would like to hear this, too.'

Jackson said, 'Is there any of your excellent ale? For this is a story to make a man thirsty and I would not like to finish before the end.'

Susannah went away and returned with a pitcher and three wooden drinking vessels. 'Wait,' she said. She disappeared again and, this time, when she returned she was holding a wooden platter of fried slices of black pudding.

'My, my,' said Jackson. 'This is a feast to behold.'

'It is in return for your tale,' said Susannah. 'Please. Speak.'

Drabble said, 'And you may begin by explaining how something that is the same can be better. For I have heard it said that Job King describes the colonies as just like England. An extension of England.'

'He does say that,' said Jackson. 'The colonies were settled by English men and women and, though others have now come there, they are still English colonies. But there are differences. Or so Job King says. And the most important difference is that, in the colonies, a man is judged by what he is and what he does and not by who his father was. If you can farm, or shoe a horse, or build a barn, you are valued. If all you can do is rule over other people and you produce nothing yourself, you are not. We would be something there and the likes of the rector and Mister Blakiston and yon Wrekin would be nothing.'

Drabble said, 'The rector and Wrekin I give you. But Blakiston is a good man. He has sometimes a rude way with him, but I don't believe he ever asked anyone to do something he could not have done himself.'

'Ay. Mebbes you are right.'

'He is right,' said Susannah. 'Mister Blakiston was a terror with me when Margaret Laws was murdered, but you cannot question his ability. And he loves Kate Greener, and his way of showing it is to make an honest woman of her. Not like the way Wrekin treated her sister.'

'I have said aye,' said Jackson. 'But he has got into his head the idea that the death of Daniel Dobson was something to do with me, and he won't let go of it. I believe the man would see me on the end of a rope, just like that man Wale and Mary Stone.'

'You could end that,' said Drabble, 'by telling him what happened to Dan Dobson. And you could tell us at the same time, for I swear you never have yet. But the Americas. What you say sounds like a miracle out of the Bible. But they still have the English King, do they not? And the English King is no friend of you and me.'

'Aye,' said Jackson. 'But Job King says that will not last for ever. He says the colonists are tired of being ordered around by the court in London. They are like us, man – they make wealth for those who already have too much, and those who already have too much take it away from them. Job King says the men and women who first went to the colonies went there so that they could be their own masters and not be beholden to those who ordered them around here. Well, Job King says their own masters under God. I think he must have found God while he was there, because I don't remember the Kings being God-fearing people while they were here.'

'So what is he saying?' asked Drabble. 'That there will be a war? And farmers and blacksmiths and builders of barns will defeat the English army?'

'Yes,' said Jackson. 'He says there will be a war and he says the colonists will win it. He also says that I would be particularly welcome there because not only can I work farm land but also I know what it is to be a soldier. But I'm afraid I am too old to go that far at my stage of life.' He looked at Susannah. 'But you… You had a reason for wanting to listen to this.'

Susannah nodded vehemently. 'Jemmy Rayne and I are soon to be wed. Jemmy's farm is small. Enclosures are not complete around Haltwhistle, where he farms, and he is afraid that the Bishop and the Blacketts want to see small farms joined together into big farms, and he might be thrown off the land. If he sold what belongs to him – his cattle, his pigs and his share of the harvest – he would have just enough to pay our fare to Virginia and live the first year while he established himself.'

'This is not idle talk,' said Drabble. 'You and he have talked about this. You mean to carry it out.'

'As I said before,' said Jackson, 'you and me should have done it at the same time as Job King. When we were young, like Susannah here and Jemmy Rayne are now. We are little better than slaves here. Every time I see that damn rector I feel like cursing him. Why should the likes of us slave the way we do and yet still go hungry while the likes of him do nothing at all and live like lords? It is wrong. I am tired of touching my forelock and bowing my head and standing back to let others go before me. Others who, without my work and yours, could never put a meal on the table, and yet they never feel the pinch of hunger while you and me are rarely sure where we will get our next meal.'

'I suppose,' said Drabble, 'that that is why you have eaten more than half of the black pudding. In any case, what have you told Job King? Have you said you will go with him?'

'I have said I will not. I am too old. And too tired. But most of the others will go. Including Ann Forman, the woman Job King rescued from the overseers of the poor.'

'Has she had her bairn yet?' asked Susannah.

'She had not when I left there. Or, at least, if she had I had not heard of it. But she may have had it now and if she has not, she will be delivered at any moment.'

'That was a good thing Job King did,' said Susannah. 'He must be a very good man.'

'Yes,' said Jackson. I believe he is.'

Drabble said, 'But not good enough, from what I hear, to give employment to William Snowball.'

'He did not. He gathered us together and said Blakiston had asked him whether he had room for Snowball and he asked what we thought. And all were agreed. Snowball would be nothing but trouble. And so Job King refused him.'

Chapter 23

And now it was Sunday. Not any Sunday. THE Sunday. The banns had been read for the first time on the second of September. Today was the twenty-third of September and today Kate Greener would become Kate Blakiston.

What had happened on the two previous Sundays could not happen today. Blakiston could not collect Kate from Chopwell Garth and carry her to church. If this had been a wedding in the style that Blakiston's class was accustomed to, it would have taken place separately from all other church activities and tradition would have dictated that Blakiston could not be permitted to see his bride before she arrived at the church. He, therefore, would have to be there before her.

There was another kind of wedding which was also carried out separately from normal church services, but it was used for the most part by couples who were marrying in secret and did not wish their families to know about the ceremony until it had been concluded.

Blakiston wanted none of that. What was most important to him was that the whole world should see his choice of bride and know that this was his decision. He therefore chose to follow the custom of the parish by marrying at the end of the Sunday service – but he accepted the opinion of his brother Peter and Kate's sister Lizzie, reinforced by the rector's wife, Lady Isabella, that he and Kate should arrive separately. Since the wife of a rector could not express such a thought in clear English to a man other than her husband, Lady Isabella's views were passed on to Blakiston by Thomas. 'Your bride comes to the altar a virgin. There will be many in the congregation who do not believe that.'

'I give not a toss about what many in the congregation choose to believe.'

'And that is to your credit, my good man. Nevertheless, allow the girl to appear as undefiled as in fact she is. You will take your place in the church early. She will come later, in the company of her sister and her sister's husband as well as her mother and other members of the family. She will not join you in the Estate's pew. Instead, she will sit towards the rear of the church.'

'But that area is reserved for common people with no right to a pew of their own!'

'Precisely so, James. And so she will be seen to be making the upward move in society that, in fact, actually is her lot. She will not join you until I have called on you to stand before me at the altar. You will have your groomsman with you; who is to give Kate away? Her father is dead, is he not?'

'You know he is, Thomas. I suppose Ned will do it. He is her younger brother, but her older brother is somewhere in the American colonies and might be unwise to present himself in Ryton, even if he could get here in time.'

'Is there still a warrant out for his arrest?'

'I don't believe any of us wishes to risk that possibility. In any case, I agree to your proposal. You have conducted many marriages; this is my first. It is my fervent hope that I shall never need to go through another.'

And so it was. The service passed as normal and differed from the conduct of other Sundays only in one particular: that Susannah Bent, who had wished to win Blakiston for herself and considered her rival unworthy of the prize, stalked from the church with her nose in the air moments before Claverley could call for James and Peter to stand before him.

'I, Kate, take thee James, to my wedded husband, to have and to hold from this day forward, for better for worse, for richer for poorer, in sickness and in health, to love, cherish, and to obey, till death us do part, according to God's holy ordinance; and thereto I give thee my troth.' Just to speak the words left Kate breathless. After all her concerns and doubts, they had reached this point.

She knew, because he saw his lips moving, that James made a vow in almost the same words, with the exception that he did not promise to obey, but all of this seemed to be happening on a plane somewhere above them.

They were married. Man and wife. This man she loved so much, and who on occasion had irritated her beyond measure, was now her husband. And she was his wife.

Then the rector stepped forward and addressed the congregation with what must surely have been the worst kept secret in Ryton for the past hundred years. There would be a celebratory repast in the rectory's barn and all were invited. Kate suspected that that was the reason so many parishioners had stayed on to the very end. She also suspected it was why Susannah Bent had removed herself – she could not have born to take part in a celebration of Blakiston's nuptials. This idea was strengthened when Susannah's mother embraced her, kissed her on the cheek and said, 'I cannot join you in a meal, but I wish you every joy in the life to come. I'm sure you understand why it is impossible for me to stay.'

Lady Isabella had done them proud in the meal that she had prepared with the assistance of Walter Wilson, the butcher, and her cook, Rosina. If there had been a single person in the church who had not known in advance that they were to be invited to eat, the smell of a whole hog turning on a spit above a fire would surely have alerted them to the idea that something was happening. There were also chickens, and trestle tables laden down with vegetable dishes and puddings.

Jeffrey Drabble and Dick Jackson set about the spread with enthusiasm. Drabble, gnawing on a chunk of pork from the pig's hindquarters, said, 'By God, I wish I still had my teeth.'

'Over there,' said Jackson. 'By where we came in. Mumbles.'

And it was true: four-day old loaves of bread had been sliced up and covered in vegetables and meat that had been chopped fine and doused in gravy so that the bread became soft enough for the toothless to eat. 'Later,' said Drabble. 'Mebbes. I can just about tear this to pieces between my gums. It's the best piece of meat I've eaten in a while.'

Jackson said, 'It would take a lot to be better than yon amlet we got at Hope House.'

While Dick and Jeffrey were gumming their way through the overloaded tables, Blakiston was speaking to Tom Laws. 'Tom. Did you think about what I asked you?'

'You mean Emmett Batey, Master?'

'I have just married your sister-in-law, Tom. If you can't call me anything but master now, I don't suppose you ever will. But, yes, I mean Emmett Batey.'

'Well, Mister Blakiston, if I can't have Joseph there – and I know I can't have Joseph there – then Emmett Batey will do well.'

'Thank you. That was what I wanted to hear. And now, you must get to your meal before all of this disappears, for I think we are watching some of the hungriest people in three counties.'

'Hungriest or greediest, sir.'

'Hungriest, Tom. Let us not be rude about our fellows on a day of such happiness.'

Kate, too, was enjoying a private conversation, hard though it was to keep at bay all those seeking to congratulate her. She was talking to Rosie Miller.

'I can't tell you how glad I was,' said Rosie, 'when my mother said you had called.'

'I was afraid you would be insulted.'

'Oh, Kate, I hope you know me better than that. Although I had better learn not to call you Kate. You must be Mistress, from now on. Or Mistress Blakiston.'

'Not when we are alone, Rosie. And not when there is only you, me and my husband.' It was the first time she had referred to Blakiston as "my husband," and she felt a shiver as she uttered the words. 'As for the rest – well, we shall see. But you are free to begin today? Tonight?'

Rosie laughed. 'Not tonight, my lady. For you are also someone else's lady, and I believe that tonight he will want you to himself.'

Though Blakiston had not told her what his brother had said, this was the same reason as Peter had given James for putting up at the inn instead of staying with them. The desire to give them privacy on their first night together as man and wife. As Kate understood what Rosie was saying, she blushed. The blush intensified when Rosie said, 'You may find yourself shouting out. I should not like it to be my presence in the house that prevented you.' And she laughed. 'But I shall be at your door early tomorrow morning, eager to begin work.' She held up an admonishing finger. 'And if I find that you have done anything that should be mine to do, then I will be cross. And you will know that I am cross. You are a lady now, Kate. You owe it to your husband not to forget that.'

In fact, it was to be some time before the night that Rosie had foretold came to pass, because Lady Isabella's hospitality extended to the new bride and groom well beyond the meal in the barn.

When the last screvige of pork and chicken had been eaten and the last parishioner had departed, Kate and Blakiston were escorted to the rectory's parlour. It was almost midnight when they walked the short distance to Kate's new home.

Blakiston held Kate at arm's length. 'Kate. My love. It is later than we could have intended. I shall understand if...' The words tailed away, but the meaning was clear. He spoke with great tenderness, but also with longing. Kate said, 'Late it may be, my husband, but the day is not yet complete. I should like to beg five minutes to myself, and then I shall expect you in my bed. And in my arms.'

Later that night, Kate snuggled against Blakiston snoring quietly beside her and listened to the sound of an owl hunting in the dark. Life could be a hard thing, as some poor field mouse or songbird at rest on a twig might be about to learn – but it could also be more wonderful than anyone could imagine. Warm in the lee of a man who she saw for the first time as naked as she was herself, she thanked God for hers.

Chapter 24

For all the glories of Sunday, the following day was a normal workday. The maid came from the inn with breakfast for two instead of one, and Kate thanked her and said that the service would not be required again. Kate would be providing breakfast for her husband and herself. And Rosie Miller arrived soon afterwards and eased Kate away from the fire. 'Seeing to that is my job, Mistress. I'll thank you to let me do it.'

And then Blakiston, having eaten his breakfast and kissed his wife (though, in his confusion at his new states, he might have been forgiven for getting those two actions the other way round), left to ensure that Lord Ravenshead's interests were being attended to as his Lordship would wish. And Kate for the first time examined the reality of the life of a wife of the gentry.

'I've nothing to do. With you here, and refusing to let me touch a thing, I've nothing to do.'

Rosie Miller said, 'Should you not be calling on the other well-born ladies of the neighbourhood?' Seeing the look of scorn on Kate's face, she giggled and went on, 'Perhaps you could start with Susannah Bent?'

'Don't. I really believe that woman hates me.'

'I really believe you're right. But you can't sit around doing nothing all day long. You have to be brought up to that, and you have not been. No-one ever taught you to paint, or to embroider, or to play the harpsichord.'

'I believe that harpsichords are no longer the thing in fashionable households. There is now something called the square piano. But, in any case, we have no such article.'

'And how do you know about the square piano? Because you can read, Kate. And that is something I cannot do. Have you no books? If not, you must get some.'

'You are right. I must.'

'And, in the meantime, perhaps you could call at Chopwell Garth. I believe you will find the people there to your liking?'

Kate laughed. 'Yes. And if I go there, they will let me do the things I'm used to doing. Keeping the place clean. Preparing meals. Looking after little Lulu. All the things that you would prevent me from doing here.'

'Apart from Lulu,' said Rosie, 'because there is no babe here. Though I imagine that you and the Master have plans to alter that.'

Kate laughed again. She had, however, something to concern herself with after all, for one of Walter Maughan's men brought a message for

James. Kate went to the door of the house. Two or three children of message carrying age were visible and Kate knew the people of Ryton well enough to choose the most reliable boy. She pressed a penny into his hand. 'You must find my husband. Mister Blakiston – you know him.'

The boy nodded. 'Yes, ma'am.'

'I don't know where he is, so you must ask until you find someone who has seen him. When you find him, tell him that Mister Maughan has prepared the list he asked for. If you get that message to him before midday, come back here and tell me so and there will be another penny for you. And doubt not that my husband will also reward you.' She smiled. 'You will be rich!'

'Thank you, ma'am. I shall give it to my mother.'

As the boy hurried away, Kate nodded to herself. He would give her penny, and any other pennies he earned, to his mother. Of course he would. It would be so good if he could keep something for himself – but the poor here learned early in their lives the importance of money. Two or three pennies earned by a child could be the difference between going to bed fed and going there hungry.

The boy was back before midday. 'Ma'am, Mister Blakiston says thank you, but he cannot visit Mister Maughan until tomorrow. I am to go to Mister Maughan now, and tell him.' He gazed at her expectantly.

'Of course. And you have come back before midday to tell me, and so you must have the penny I promised you.' She gave it to him. 'Did my husband also give you a penny?'

'Yes, thank you, ma'am.'

'That is good. And I make no doubt that Mister Maughan will do the same and so you will have four pence to give to your mother. She will be very pleased.'

And the boy hurried off. It would take him some time to reach Walter Maughan's farm. He would have earned those four pennies hard. She was glad to note that he had been barefoot, for it would not be to anyone's advantage to earn money while wearing out the soles of his shoes. And then she caught herself. How could she possibly be thinking that it was good that the boy had no shoes? It was already the end of September. Winter was not far away. He would need more than his bare feet then to see him through the cold.

And now she was back with the same problem that she had already discussed with Rosie: filling her time. And then she realised that she had a man to look after. There must be a meal waiting for him tonight and, as yet, she had nothing in the house to feed him on. She had told the girl from the inn that she would look after future breakfasts. With what?

She took a basket and set off for Chopwell Garth. She could call later on Walter Wilson, the butcher, and Adam Manners, the greengrocer – but first she would find out what Florrie and Lizzie could sell her in the way of eggs, bacon, cheese, black pudding, milk and whatever else they might have for sale.

Blakiston had his midday meal at an inn on the far side of the village. When he got home, he was tired and ready to eat but the first thing he wanted was simply to hold his new wife close to him. Then she took his hat and coat from him and encouraged him to sit close to the fire. She hung up the coat and hat, making a mental note to brush them before he put them on again and then she knelt before him and pulled off his boots. She looked up. 'Tell me about your day.'

And so he did – and as he described all the humdrum and tedious details of the past ten hours, he was as astonished by her interest as she was by ownership of it. They both knew that this was an interest that would diminish with time, but for now everything about their lives together was new and fascinating.

And then they had dinner, and Kate had to accept that it didn't matter that you had known the maid since you were both toddling babes: the maid had her own space and did not share yours. Kate would talk to Rosie the next day and suggest that, when she wasn't actually working, her mother might welcome her company and she might welcome her mother's. This business of hiring your oldest friend was not as simple as it might have seemed.

Chapter 25

After dinner, when Rosie had cleared away the dishes and was washing them in the scullery, Kate said, 'James. Today is Monday and I believe Joseph Laws was to be released from jail.'

'That is so, my love.'

'You are satisfied that he did not kill his wife?'

'I am certain that he did not kill Ezra Hindmarsh, because he could not have done so. He was in jail when the boy died. And whoever killed Ezra Hindmarsh also killed Margaret Laws.'

'Very well. It was not Joseph. But it was someone – so, if not Joseph, who?'

'That, my dear, is something I do not yet know.'

'And also why? In fact, is that not the most important question?'

'Do you say so?'

'Well, someone killed Margaret Laws and they had a reason for doing it. Is that not so? No-one kills another person for no reason, surely?'

The thought that had been concerning Blakiston to the point where it frightened him was precisely that – that there might be, loose in Ryton, someone who killed for no reason other than the pleasure of killing. But he did not want to say that to the woman he loved most in all the world – a woman, after all, all of whose family lived in Ryton. He therefore simply nodded.

'Well,' said Kate, 'how many reasons can there be? Why does one person kill another?'

'It seems to me that the number of reasons must be as large as the number of people in the world.'

'But, James. Is that really so? I can think of three men who have been killed in Ryton while I have been old enough to know about it. I mean, apart from Matthew Higson, whose killer you found and so the reason for whose murder we know. All three were killed by drink.'

'They drank themselves to death?'

'They might as well have done. They drank so much they lost their senses and so did someone drinking with them, and that someone picked up a stool or a jug or at least something and dashed their brains out. Why? They could never say. Something the dead person had said while drunk. Some insult the person who killed suddenly remembered from days long past. Something that had never happened, for the person who killed was so drunk he had imagined it. And the killer's name was known immediately because he sat there in his stupor until the constable arrived to take him to the lock-up. When Richard Brown killed his daughter by throwing her down a well, he was so drunk he did not even know he had done it. He was so repentant. But still they hanged him on Newcastle Town Moor.'

'I think we can be sure that whoever killed Margaret Laws and Ezra Hindmarsh did not do so because of drink.'

'Mary Stone killed Reuben Cooper because she wanted the money he was reputed to have. And then she killed Matthew Higson because she was afraid he knew what she had done and would tell people. Margaret Laws had no money, but it might be interesting to find out whether she knew a secret that someone would kill to protect.'

'You are right, my love, and if it were not for Ezra Hindmarsh then that would be a good thing to enquire into.'

'Because he was just a boy? A boy of Ezra's age can know someone else's secret as well as a woman of Margaret's.'

Blakiston poured himself another glass of wine. Kate was right, of course. But there was the matter he had under suspicion. The matter that involved the list prepared by Walter Maughan. Should he voice his suspicions? He knew that he should, because Kate's intelligence and ability to see through to the essence of a matter had helped him bring the killers of Reuben Cooper and Matthew Higson to justice. But it was not quite that simple, because there was a maid in the house and anything she heard might be passed on and become public knowledge. He did not want that, because he did not want to put the murderer on notice. He lowered his voice. Kate, understanding why he did so, leaned forward to hear what he had to say.

'This list that Walter Maughan has prepared for me.'

'Yes? I assumed that that was a matter of his Lordship's business.'

'It is not. What Maughan has produced is a list of every pauper whose case was ever discussed by him, the older Ezra Hindmarsh, and Wilkin Longstaff acting together.'

Kate stared at him. 'Maughan. Hindmarsh. Longstaff. They have all been overseers of the poor?'

'They have.'

'Maughan's daughter was murdered. Hindmarsh's grandson, too. And Wilkin Longstaff's grand daughter believes that she was watched by someone who intended her ill.'

'Just so.'

'Revenge is a motive for murder that we did not discuss.'

'It is.'

'And you suspect that revenge is at work here.'

'I do.'

'You suspect, in fact, that the killer knew paupers who died, and holds the overseers responsible.'

'I think it possible.'

'When will you see this list of Walter Maughan's?'

'Not today, for today is almost over. And not tomorrow, because I have received a message that Lord Ravenshead wishes to see me, and that must take priority over all.'

'On Wednesday, then?'

'I hope so.'

'Then we must wait.' She picked up one of Blakiston's hands in both of hers. How large it seemed in comparison with her own. 'But not everything requires that we wait.'

Blakiston smiled. 'Did you have something particular in mind?'

'I did.' She let go of his hand, picked up the bottle and filled his glass. 'I should like you, my love, to drink this glass of wine. Not quickly, but not slowly, either.'

Blakiston's smile grew wider. 'And while I am drinking it? What will you be doing?'

'I shall be upstairs, readying myself for bed.' She leaned over and kissed him on the forehead. 'And when you have finished your wine, I should like you to join me there.'

With that, she rose from her chair and walked towards the stairs. Blakiston watched, suffused by a feeling of absolute contentment.

Chapter 26

Tuesday was 25 September and the cold wind left no-one in any doubt that summer had departed, autumn was following it and winter would soon be here. When Thomas Claverley went into Holy Cross Church, he was wrapped against the cold on the instructions of Lady Isabella, his wife. 'You could freeze in that place, Thomas. It is cold and it will be colder.'

Thomas already knew that the church had a visitor, because he had observed the horse outside. It was something of a surprise to see that the visitor was Job King for, although King had visited once before outside the hours of services and although he was scrupulous in being there at the set time each Sunday, Thomas thought that King's faith was probably only slightly less absent than Blakiston's. He was about to learn that he was wrong. The estate King was renting had of course its own pew and King was sitting there. Thomas sat beside him but said nothing.

After a few minutes, King said, 'Rector. I have been waiting for you.'

'Yes?'

'I thought at one point that I would be waiting for you for a different purpose. But that is something I now find I lack the heart to put into practice and, in any case, you were not the man.' Claverley said nothing. Clearly, King had something to say to him and he would get there or he would not. Some more minutes passed and then King said, 'I would like you to hear my confession. But first there is a question I must ask you.'

The rector said, 'Confession is not something often practised in this church. We regard it – I regard it – as having something of the papist about it. Nevertheless, if you must tell it to me, I must hear it. What is your question?'

'My understanding is that you can never tell anyone what I confess to you. However wicked or sinful it may be. Is that correct?'

'Confession is a sacrament, as holy as the Eucharist or any other sacrament. Whatever you tell me must remain between us. I could not break your confidence even to prevent a crime.'

'Or to punish one?'

'Or for that.'

'And does this apply in all cases? Even if someone confesses to you that they have committed the ultimate crime and sin of murder, you are bound never to tell a living soul?'

'Even then. But, King, I can see that you are in extreme agony. Let us begin. Make the sign of the cross. Come, come, the days of the puritans are gone. You will not be cast into hell for the simple matter of moving your fingers in the shape of a cross. Rather the reverse, in fact. There, you see? Now, say these words: Bless me, Father, for I have sinned.'

When King had spoken those words, the rector said, 'Now. You do not need to tell me what you have done, for there have only been two murders since you arrived in this parish. What I should like you to do is not to tell me what, for it is clear that it was you who killed Margaret Laws and Ezra Hindmarsh. I should like you, King, to tell me why.'

'You were not here in this parish when I was a boy. And so you will not remember. But I had two brothers and two sisters. My father was a hard-working man. A labourer, who worked his own strips on the common and worked on farms belonging to the Bishop or his Lordship when that work was available. My mother was a good woman, who took in washing for the gentry of the parish and cleaned their houses when they asked. She kept chickens and my father kept a pig. We were poor by the standards of such as you, Rector, but we never went hungry, we were always tidily dressed and we knew our gospel stories.

'And then came the influenza. My father died on Friday; my mother followed him on Sunday; and we five fell into the charge of the overseers of the poor. I do not know what happened to the chickens, Rector. I do not know what happened to the pig. We were told that the money they brought would be placed to our account but the fact is that from that moment on we were never anything but hungry, and our clothes turned to rags and were never replaced. The one thing that did not change from when my mother and father were alive was that we still found ourselves in church every Sunday. This time, we were chased there by your predecessor and told to spend the time thanking God for his mercies. And one by one my brothers and sisters starved to death.'

The rector had remained silent throughout this confession. Now he said, 'And for this you blame…?'

'Walter Maughan was one of the overseers at that time. Walter Maughan is always one of the overseers. Ezra Hindmarsh – that is, the older Ezra Hindmarsh – was another. The others do not matter now, because when I began I believed that taking one each from the four who had taken four from me would bring me relief.'

'It did not?'

'It brought me pain beyond any imagining. I have committed a sin that can never be forgiven. I am damned for all eternity. I know that.' He raised his eyes for the first time to look at Claverley. 'And you, Rector, have listened to me with patience. You have not for one moment looked as though you judged me. And yet now your face says that I have angered you.'

'It is not for you, King, to say that you are eternally damned, and nor is it for me. Every one of us – every man, every woman and every child on this earth – is damned, thanks to the sin of Adam and Eve. But God is merciful. I do not know and you do not know whether his mercy will be extended to you, but I do know that you took the second step towards obtaining it when you came here to open your heart – to me, but also to God.'

'Second step? What was the first?'

'The first step was the mercy you showed to Ann Forman. Without you, she and her child would be subject to the same fate as you have described for your brothers and sisters. You saved her from it.'

'He answereth and saith unto them, He that hath two coats, let him impart to him that hath none; and he that hath meat, let him do likewise.'

'Thanks be to God. The gospel according to Luke. I believe that Luke was closer to the spirit of Christ than any of the other Gospels. But you do not speak those words as one who learned them by rote in this church when you were a child.'

'When I left these shores, Rector, I had abandoned all ideas of faith. Living among the colonists has restored much of what I once had from my mother and father.'

'I had heard that faith in God is stronger now in the colonies than at home.'

'You have heard right.'

'Before you made your confession, you were determined to know that I could tell no-one about it. I take it, then, that it is not your intention to throw yourself on the mercy of the Law.'

'It is not.'

'I am bound to ask whether you do not see that that may be what God wants you to do.'

'I have disappointed God many times, Rector. I am content to do it once more. It will be bad enough to stand before Him on the day of my death. I do not intend to compound that by swinging at the end of a rope for a law that is made only by man and for the benefit of those much richer than I when that same law was snuffing out the lives of my brothers and sisters like fluttering candles.'

'Then the only thing remaining to me, King, is to tell you that you are absolved, insofar as God's human representative can achieve that. Go in peace. And take care to sin no more.'

Chapter 27

The next morning, Blakiston set off for his meeting with Lord Ravenshead. The welcome was cordial as ever – more so, in fact, as Lord Ravenshead wished to congratulate Blakiston on his marriage. 'I take it none of the Blackett family put in an appearance?'

Blakiston smiled. He knew his Lordship's views about the Blacketts and he understood that no reply was needed. His Lordship said, 'The harvest went well?'

'According to the records, it was easily the best we have ever had. Of course, the weather was kind to us this year. It rained when we would have it rain and the sun shone when the grain was already full in the ear.'

'Yes, Blakiston, the weather contributed – but your care and your introduction of new scientific methods contributed even more. You will find that I have authorised an additional payment to you. It is partly because you are now a married man with a wife who has a wife's needs, but it is mostly a sign of my gratitude for the improvements you have made in this estate.'

'Thank you, your Lordship.'

'It is no more than you deserve, Blakiston. You have heard that Job King intends to return to the colonies?'

'I had.'

'I wondered, Blakiston, whether you had ever considered a move to the colonies yourself?'

Blakiston pondered his reply. He was not going to say that the thought had never crossed his mind, because that would not have been true. In fact, the truth was something to which he could give voice now. 'It was very much in my mind, your Lordship. But then I was offered this position here. If you had not taken me on, I imagine I would be in Virginia at this moment.'

'Then this country is as fortunate as I am that I made my offer when I did. But, Blakiston. The estate that King has been renting. What do you know of it?'

'I have dined there as a guest of Job King. It is a pretty house, well furnished and appointed. It has attractive gardens of its own and it is at the heart of fertile farm land that has done well for King, was doing well before him, and could do even better in the future.'

'I am pleased to hear you say that. My son... Wrekin. He shows as yet no sign of wishing to settle and I confess that when I think of a suitable mate for him, no name presses itself forward. His wife, when he takes one, will have to be a woman of good family, of at least equal rank with our own and ideally higher. She will also need to bring with her a significant endowment. But that, as I say, is still in the future. The fact is, Blakiston – and I should prefer that this not be spoken about outside these walls – that I and my son make do not find it easy to live in the same house. It would be better for his equilibrium were he to be established in a place of his own. And it would certainly be better for mine. What I wondered, Blakiston, is whether the estate that King will be vacating might be a suitable place for him. It is far enough away for us not to be forever in each other's way and close enough that I would hear regularly of his doings there. What do you think?'

Blakiston's opinion of Wrekin was a poor one. Blakiston, along with the rector, had had to deal with the after effects of Wrekin's ravishing of Lizzie Greener. They had done so and done it well, and the result was not only the raising of Tom Laws but also the chain of events that had ended with Blakiston's marriage to Kate. Nevertheless, Blakiston had not failed to notice that Wrekin had taken no part at all in covering the damage cause by what had, however you looked at it, been an act of rape. In fact, he had seemed to feel that the storm he had bought about his ears was a fuss about nothing. He had dishonoured a girl from the lower orders – his attitude could perhaps be best described as, "So what?"

But none of that would have been well received by Ravenshead. And so Blakiston said that what he thought: that not only would the estate be a good place for his Lordship to place his son, but it would also be an excellent investment and likely to return a tidy profit over the years.

Ravenshead clapped his hands. 'That is excellent. I confess it is exactly what I hoped to hear. But we will keep it between ourselves, Blakiston. What? '

'We should certainly do that, your Lordship, until you have been able to accomplish the purchase. There is nothing to be gained by putting the vendors on notice that you have an interest there.'

'My thoughts exactly. I shall have my agent recruit the services of another agent so that the presence of Ravenshead money in the transaction will not be obvious until terms have been agreed.'

His business with Lord Ravenshead having concluded earlier than he had expected, Blakiston found that he could now call on Walter Maughan that afternoon instead of the following day. When he arrived, they went through the social routine to which he was by now resigned in Maughan's company. He was shown into the parlour. Coffee, fruit cake and cheese were served. And then Maughan placed the list before him. He said, 'I do not know what you can learn from this, because it is certain that I have learned nothing from it myself, but I have been through the records of all three chapelries with great care and I am sure that every pauper that was dealt with by me, Ezra Hindmarsh and Wilkin Longstaff together is on that list.'

Blakiston surveyed the names. Then he folded the list, placed it into a pocket in his jacket, and stood up. 'Thank you, Maughan. I shall study it with care and see whether it speaks any more clearly to me than it does to you.'

When he got home that evening, he placed the list in front of his wife. 'Walter Maughan says he can see no pattern in these names. I wonder whether you will agree with him.'

Over dinner, Kate said, 'It seems to me that the pattern is very clear. And it points at only one name.'

'Yes,' said Blakiston. 'That is what I thought. And the name in question is that of Job King.'

Kate nodded. 'There was a fourth overseer with them. Ezekiel Watson. And he has grandchildren.'

'They will be in danger. As will Matilda Longstaff. They must be protected. He must know that he is identified.'

'What will you do?'

'I shall confront him with the evidence and ask what he has to say for himself.'

Chapter 28

It would not have been Blakiston's way to postpone dealing with an uncomfortable situation, and he did not do so. The following morning, he presented himself at the imposing entrance to Job King's residence. Told that King was still at breakfast, Blakiston said, 'I shall wait. You may inform your master that this is not a social visit.'

The man showed Blakiston into a room in which he was to wait and hurried away. He was quickly back. 'If you will come this way, Mister Blakiston, Mister King will be happy to see you.'

Blakiston was shown into what was clearly a breakfast room and found King enjoying a substantial meal. 'Thank you, Jonathan,' said King. 'You may leave us. Please close the door and make sure that everyone knows that Mister Blakiston and I are not to be interrupted.' He looked at Blakiston and the overseer was unable to avoid the conclusion that King was smiling at him. 'Mister Blakiston. You will take breakfast with me?'

'Thank you, but no. I ate handsomely just before coming here.'

King nodded. 'Take a seat, man, at least. And you will excuse me if I finish my own meal.' He gathered a piece of fried egg onto a piece of bacon, put both onto a piece of bread and placed the whole in his mouth. Still the impression of a hidden smile was irresistibly there. He said, 'You have something you wish to ask me, I believe.'

'Walter Maughan. Wilkin Longstaff. Ezra Hindmarsh. Do those names together have any significance for you?'

'You have missed one.'

'I beg your pardon?'

'Walter Maughan. Wilkin Longstaff. Ezra Hindmarsh. And Isaac Oliver. All four were overseers of the poor and all four allowed my two brothers and two sisters to starve to death.'

'You killed Margaret Laws and the young Ezra Hindmarsh.'

'An eye for an eye,' Mister Blakiston. 'A life for a life.'

'You admit it?'

'Aye, to you, with no-one else listening. I wish you well with the knowledge; you have no witnesses to my confession and if you attempt to bring me before a judge the judge will see that I am richer than you, and of greater importance, and you will not be believed. That is the way of it in England. You might be listened to more closely in the colonies. But that is not where we are.'

Blakiston leaned forward and banged his fist on the table. 'You are confessing to murder. And yet you expect to go unpunished. What sort of world is this?'

'The sort our betters have made for us. It worked against me and mine when we were young; forgive me if I choose to make use of it now.'

'That is detestable!'

'More detestable than the negligence of the overseers who let my brothers and sisters die? Those Christian men who gave praise and thanks to God in church every Sunday and showed my family no mercy?'

Blakiston sat back in his chair. There was no point in allowing anger to get the better of him. He knew now who the killer was and he knew he could do nothing about it.

King said, 'I have been expecting your visit. I am grateful, for it allows me to say what I want to say.'

'You intended to kill Matilda Longstaff.'

'I did. And when I had done so, I meant to kill Isaac Oliver's grandson Reuben.'

'Why did you not do so? Why did you spare the Longstaff girl?'

'Because, my dear fellow, it was not as I expected. I have brooded for years over the wrongs done to my family. I have dreamed of the satisfaction that righting those wrongs would bring me. It did not. I killed Margaret Laws and it brought me no satisfaction and no peace. I killed the Hindmarsh boy and that was worse because there was still no satisfaction and no peace and now I had the pain of seeing how much hurt I had visited on the old man and his wife. Hindmarsh did me and my family great wrong. What I learned was that there was no comfort in doing him wrong in return.'

'And Matilda Longstaff?'

'I could not do it. It was as simple as that. I saw her there, I had it in my power to inflict on Wilkin Longstaff the same hurt as I had on Ezra Hindmarsh, but by now I knew that I could take no pleasure from it. I did not even look at Reuben Oliver. Four of my brothers and sisters died because of those four men. Killing Matilda Longstaff and Reuben Oliver would not have avenged the four of mine. It would simply have meant that two more children were dead. Two more young people who could have lived lives in which who knows what they might have achieved? I could not do it. When wrong has been done to you by others, you do not make it right by doing wrong yourself. You simply add to the total of wrongs that have been done. I did not understand that, and now I do. I was as helpless to achieve vengeance as you are to do anything with this knowledge you now have.' He drank the last of his tea, wiped his beard and moustache with a napkin and stood up. 'And now, Mister Blakiston, I am returning to the colonies with all of those who depend on me. I take my guilt with me, for God to deal with in His own good time. Your impotence to see me punished I shall leave with you. This is not the best time to sail across the Atlantic, but I have decided that we will go now because I wish to be far from the scene of my wrongdoing as soon as possible. I do know it for what it is. I am not prepared to stand before a human judge and answer for it. I shall face the judgement of God soon enough, and I fear it. I bid you good day, Mister Blakiston.'

And he walked from the room, untouchable. In his fury, Blakiston picked up a cup and hurled it at the wall, but no-one came to see what was causing the noise. When he felt calm enough at least to conceal his rage, he walked through the building and out of the door he had entered by. One of King's men was holding Obsidian. Blakiston took the reins from him without a word, leapt into the saddle and turned towards the road. He glanced for a moment at the footman. He could swear that the man's face bore the same hidden amusement as his master's.

Chapter 29

It fell to Kate to try to rouse her husband from his despair. 'My love. Job King has done wrong…'

'He has *killed*!'

'Yes, he has killed. He has done wrong. And one day he will face God's justice, and he knows it. We may be sure that he will be dealt with to the last degree of his sinfulness.'

'That is as may be, but my concern is with Man's justice, not God's, and that he will not face.'

'My love. Forgive me. But you are from a class that expects Man's justice to be done and I am not. When Wrekin did what he did to my sister, he was not punished. Lizzie gained and I gained and Tom Laws gained, but nothing was done to Wrekin. He was too rich, too well born and too powerful.'

'And do you think, Kate, that that is God's will?'

'I cannot see that it can be otherwise, for if it were not God's will, then how would He allow it to happen?'

Blakiston glowered. 'I should have been able to take him before the Assize. He should stand trial for what he has done.'

'And he will not. When he was Job King the pauper, he would have gone on trial.'

'He would have *hung*!'

'But now he is Job King the rich man, and unless he offends against someone even richer, he cannot be touched. That is the way of this world. And God must want it, or God would not permit it.'

'Really, Kate, I don't know what I should do if I did not have you here with me.'

'And that, my love, is why God allowed us to come together, separated by class and the ways of man though we were.'

Bit by bit, Blakiston allowed himself to think of other things. He reported to Lord Ravenshead on what he could learn about the estate Job King was vacating, and Ravenshead employed an agent to buy it on behalf of Wrekin. Job King left the neighbourhood and then the country with all his dependents. Jeffrey Drabble and Dick Jackson wondered what kind of lives they might have led had they had the courage to go to the colonies as King had done. Susannah Ward married Jemmy Rayne, Rayne sold everything he had, and they embarked on the same vessel as Job King. The last thing Susannah said to Kate was, 'The captain has warned us that the weather will be bad and the crossing rough. But we don't have enough money to support ourselves here until the spring and still buy a passage to the colonies and keep us there until Jemmy is established. And, because of the weather, passage is cheaper now than it will be in spring.'

Three weeks later, Blakiston returned home much earlier than was normal on a working day and placed a newspaper in front of Kate without saying a word. His finger pointed to an article headed, "Disaster at Sea." Kate read it. Then, tears clouding her eyes, she read it again.

She looked up at Blakiston. 'No-one was saved.'

'It seems not.'

'Poor Susannah. And Jemmy – he was Tom's cousin. And Ann Foreman with her bairn.'

'And Job King.'

Kate pushed the paper away from her. 'And Job King. It seems he has faced God's justice sooner than he expected.'

If Blakiston had given vent to his feelings, he would have asked whether Kate thought the balance was equal. To bring Job King to stand – as Kate saw it, and Blakiston as surely did not – before an almighty God to face justice for what he had done, so many innocents with all their hopes for the future had lost their lives. Was that the way Kate thought her God operated? But he did not say a word of this, because Kate would have found it hurtful and the one constant in Blakiston's life was a determination to do nothing to hurt the woman he loved.

And yet, it seemed that Kate knew what was in his mind, because she said, 'Only God knows who is truly innocent. And all those people came from the poor of this parish and not the well off. We can be certain that the life they have now in heaven is better than anything they left behind.'

Blakiston sat down. He took both of Kate's hands in his. He turned one of her hands over, kissed it, and then closed the fingers on the kiss. 'There,' he whispered. 'Now you have a kiss with you, whenever you want it.'

Kate laughed. 'There is a sentence I have heard from the Rector at funerals. "In the midst of death, we are in life." Or, at least, that is how I think it goes – I may not be remembering it quite right.'

'And why do you mention this now, my dear?'

'Because all of these people are dead. And here, in this parish and in this house, something that should have happened has not happened.'

'Is something wrong?'

'Only if you would prefer not to be a father. I am with child. I believe it will be born in the height of summer. It will be a child of the summer and a child of joy.'

Entirely lost for words, Blakiston wrapped his arms around his wife and hugged her close to him. 'A child of joy indeed.' Was he, a man who put justice and honesty before all, prepared to accept that the price of joy must sometimes be injustice?

What choice did he have?

From The Author

I hope you enjoyed this book. In case you are not aware, let me say that it is the second book in the *James Blakiston Series* and the first was *A Just and Upright Man*. Book 3 in the series is due to be published in July 2019.

I write historical fiction in the name of RJ Lynch (my initials reversed) and I write contemporary fiction in the name of John Lynch. You might like these:

The Making of Billy McErlane. It isn't the cards you're dealt that count, but how you play the hand. Originally called *Zappa's Mam's a Slapper*, this is the story of a young man born into the family from hell who makes a success of his life against all the odds.

Sharon Wright: Butterfly. No-one gives Sharon a chance – except Sharon. Only an idiot would fall in love with Sharon, because Sharon loves the way a female mantis might – knowing that, when she's done, the male may have to die. South London is not short of idiots.

CPSIA information can be obtained
at www.ICGtesting.com
Printed in the USA
BVHW041710091122
651596BV00006B/166

9 781910 194225